CAILLEACH'S EMBRACE

also by P. Hartwell

The Last Inhale

The Sacred Island

Beneath West Seneca

Time in Kilkenny

CAILLEACH'S EMBRACE

Where Shadows Speak and Tides Remember

P. HARTWELL

CAILLEACH'S EMBRACE

Cover art and design by P. Hartwell

ISBN: 978-1-969929-06-9

Prologue

For those who find solace in wild places, attuned to the wind's whispers and the ocean's shifting tales—may your curiosity be your compass, guiding you through peril toward understanding.

This story is woven from ancient myth and the raw pulse of human emotion, a tribute to the forces that shape both land and soul. It's for those who've heard the call of the unknown, stood at the edge of the world, and felt its vastness.

For the artists who capture beauty in chaos, the seekers who chase truth through shadow, and the guardians of quiet truths. For Gladys, drawn to the spark where legend meets reality, and for Liam, the pubkeeper whose eyes reflect the sea's wisdom and who dared to confront the ghosts beneath his routine.

Let the ocean's echo resound through these pages—a reminder that some mysteries aren't solved, but felt. This tale is dedicated to the pull of the unknown and the courage to face it, even in the heart of the storm.

The moonlight falls on a remote Irish cove, waves crashing against jagged stone—a fitting stage for Cailleach's Embrace.

Chapter One - The Siren's Call

Arrival on the Emerald Isle

The air, thick with the briny embrace of the Atlantic, was Gladys Burton's first true acquaintance with Ireland. It was a scent that spoke of ages past, of salt-laced winds that had shaped these shores for millennia, and the earthy, comforting aroma of peat smoke clinging to the moist air. Inhaling deeply, she experienced a profound release, as if a burdensome husk of herself was being shed. Gone was the dissonance of the city, the relentless hum of traffic, the glare of artificial lights; replaced by a profound, almost tangible serenity broken only by the mournful cry of gulls and the rhythmic sigh of the waves against a distant, unseen shore.

The village, a scattering of whitewashed cottages huddled against the vast, indifferent sweep of the sky, felt as though it had been etched into the landscape by patient, weathered hands. It was a place where time seemed to swirl and pool, slowing to the rhythm of the tides rather than the ticking of a clock. The locals, emerging from their homes like shy sea creatures from their rocky crevices, offered a reserved but genuine welcome. Their eyes, a spectrum of blues and greys mirroring the ever-shifting hues of the ocean, held a depth that spoke of generations tethered to this wild edge of the world. There was a reserve, a quietude about them, not of unfriendliness, but of a shared understanding of the power of silence, of words held back like treasures.

Gladys, an artist whose soul pulsed with the need to translate the world onto canvas, felt an immediate kinship with this raw, untamed beauty. The urban sprawl she had fled, a concrete and steel labyrinth that had begun to suffocate her spirit, felt a lifetime away. Here, the landscape was alive, breathing with a melancholic grandeur that resonated deep within her. Her artist's eye, trained to find beauty in the mundane, was now overwhelmed by the sheer, untamed magnificence of it all. The emerald fields, impossibly vibrant against the bruised purple of the distant hills, seemed to glow with an inner light. The rugged coastline, a dramatic interplay of jagged cliffs and sweeping sands, was a masterpiece sculpted by the relentless hand of the sea.

But it was the cove, tucked away like a secret whispered between the land and the ocean, that truly captured her imagination. It drew her with an almost magnetic force, a siren's call sung not in music, but in the crash of waves and the lonely cry of the wind. Local lore, she sensed, clung to this place like the sea spray to the rocks, weaving tales of ancient beings and forgotten rites. It promised escape, yes, a balm for her frayed nerves and a respite from the ghosts of her past, but it also promised inspiration, a muse of primal power that seemed to beckon her closer. She felt a stirring within her, an artistic hunger that this place, with its wild beauty and hidden depths, was poised to sate. The very air around it seemed to thrum with an unspoken story, a narrative waiting to be uncovered, and Gladys, with her insatiable curiosity and her artist's heart, felt an irresistible urge to listen.

The journey from the relative bustle of the small airport to this remote village had been a descent into a different world. The roads narrowed, becoming winding tracks that hugged the coastline, offering tantalizing glimpses of the churning sea below. Trees, bent and gnarled by the persistent winds, seemed to bow in deference to the elements. The further she travelled, the more the modern world receded, replaced by a timeless landscape that felt both ancient and alive. The village itself, when it finally appeared, was not a picturesque postcard cliché, but something far more substantial, more grounded. Stone walls, weathered and moss-covered, delineated small, tidy plots. Smoke curled lazily from chimneys, testament to the hearths within, to lives lived in rhythm with the seasons.

Gladys's small rented cottage, perched on a gentle rise overlooking the harbor, was simple but welcoming. The interior smelled faintly of beeswax and dried lavender, and the windows framed views that stole her breath. The sea, a vast, ever-changing canvas of blues, greens, and greys, dominated the horizon. She could feel its presence even within the stone walls, a constant, murmuring reminder of the wild power that shaped this land. Unpacking her sketchbooks and charcoals, she felt a surge of anticipation, the familiar thrum of creative energy beginning to pulse within her. This was what she had come for, this escape, this immersion in a world far removed from the anxieties that had driven her across the ocean.

The first few days were a blur of sensory exploration. She walked the windswept beaches, collecting sea-smoothed pebbles and pieces of driftwood, each fragment whispering its own story of the ocean's journey. She ventured into the small village pub, a warm, dimly lit haven filled with the scent of ale and the murmur of local voices. The villagers, initially watchful, slowly began to thaw, their reserve melting into a quiet warmth as they saw her genuine appreciation for their home. They were a hardy folk, their faces etched with the stories of sun, wind, and sea, their hands calloused from a life of labor.

There was Liam, the pub owner, a man with a booming laugh and eyes that seemed to hold the wisdom of the tides. He served her a pint of the local stout, its rich, dark flavor a perfect complement to the salty air, and spoke of the village with a pride that was as deep and enduring as the ocean itself. He cautioned her, with a knowing glint in his eye, about the sea's capricious nature, its beauty and its danger intertwined. "She gives, and she takes, mind," he'd said, his voice a low rumble. "Never forget that."

Then there was Maeve, the unofficial historian, a woman whose knowledge of the local lore seemed as vast and intricate as the ancient Celtic knots carved into the standing stones scattered across the landscape. Maeve's eyes held a faraway look, as if she saw not just the present, but the echoes of centuries past. She spoke of mermaids and selkies, of shipwrecks and drowned souls, her voice weaving a tapestry of myth and memory that painted the very air with magic and a touch of ancient dread. Gladys listened, captivated, sketching furiously in her notebook, trying to capture the essence of these tales, the spectral figures that seemed to dance at the edge of her vision.

And Finn. Finn the fisherman. He was a man of few words, his presence a quiet, watchful force. She saw him mending nets down by the harbor, his movements economical and practiced, his gaze often fixed on the horizon, as if in constant conversation with the sea. Their paths crossed briefly, a shared nod, a fleeting exchange of glances. There was a depth in his eyes, a stoic resilience that suggested a profound understanding of the elements, and perhaps, of secrets best left undisturbed.

It was the cove, however, that truly possessed her. Cailleach's Embrace, they called it, a name that hinted at something ancient and powerful. The path leading to it was narrow and winding, disappearing into a tangle of gorse and heather. As she descended, the roar of the ocean intensified, the air growing cooler, heavier with moisture. The cove itself was a dramatic amphitheater carved into the coastline, its sheer cliffs rising like guardian sentinels. The water within was a shifting kaleidoscope of colors, from the deep sapphire of the ocean's depths to the pale jade of the shallows. Jagged rocks, slick with seaweed, jutted out from the water, creating treacherous channels and hidden pools.

Gladys spent hours there, perched on a high outcrop, her sketchbook open on her lap. She felt a profound connection to this place, a sense of belonging that transcended explanation. It was as if the cove itself recognized a kindred spirit in her, a fellow artist drawn to the raw, elemental beauty of the world. Her sketches, initially attempts to capture the sweep of the cliffs and the play of light on the water, began to evolve. She found herself sketching figures, spectral forms woven into the very fabric of the landscape, hints of the legends Maeve had shared. The more she looked, the more she saw, the more the cove seemed to reveal its hidden stories.

She was an observer, yes, but she also felt like a participant, drawn into the ancient narrative that played out here. The villagers watched her, she knew. Their quiet glances, the hushed conversations that ceased when she passed, were not lost on her. They saw her fascination, perhaps, as something more than mere artistic curiosity. They saw her lingering by the water's edge, her gaze fixed on the swirling currents, and they whispered their warnings, their tales of treacherous tides and the sea's unforgiving grip. But Gladys, lost in her creative trance, barely registered their unease. For her, the cove was a muse, a sanctuary, a promise of something profound and transformative. She was not seeking danger; she was seeking truth, beauty, and a connection to something larger than herself, and she believed, with a fervent artist's conviction, that she had found it here, on this wild, windswept coast. The world she had left behind was a fading memory, and the allure of Cailleach's Embrace, with its secrets and its siren song, was all that mattered. She felt herself falling, not into danger, but into a story, and she was eager to see how it would unfold.

Whispers of the Cove

The cove, a jagged scar upon the rugged Irish coastline, held a name whispered with a mixture of reverence and dread: Cailleach's Embrace. It was a moniker that clung to the place like the persistent mist, a testament to the stories that swirled around its shadowed depths, stories that had been passed down through generations, etched into the very soul of the land. Gladys, however, saw no embrace of doom. Instead, she perceived an invitation, a primal summons that resonated with the artistic fire burning within her. For her, the whispers were not of warning, but of inspiration, a haunting melody sung by the wind and waves, a siren's call that beckoned her closer to the heart of its wild, untamed beauty.

The folklore surrounding Cailleach's Embrace was as ancient and deep as the ocean itself. Maeve, the village's unofficial keeper of lore, had painted vivid, almost spectral images with her words. She spoke of mermaids, their voices like the mournful cry of the gulls, luring sailors to their watery graves. She spoke of selkies, the mythical creatures who shed their sealskins to walk upon the land, their hearts forever bound to the sea. And most poignantly, she spoke of the shipwrecks, the phantom vessels that, on moonless nights, were said to still sail the treacherous waters, their spectral crews forever reenacting their final, desperate moments. The cove, Maeve had explained, with a glint of something akin to fear in her eyes, was a place where the veil between worlds thinned, where the sea's power was raw and untamed, capable of both immense beauty and utter devastation. The treacherous tides, she had warned, were not mere currents; they were the breath of something ancient, something that could pull the unwary into its depths and never let them go.

Yet, these tales, rather than deterring Gladys, acted as a potent fuel for her imagination. She would spend hours perched on a weathered outcrop, the salty spray misting her face, her charcoal flying across the pages of her sketchbook. The swirling waters, a tempestuous dance of emerald and sapphire, captivated her. The jagged rocks, slick with emerald-green seaweed and encrusted with barnacles, seemed like ancient teeth bared against the relentless surge of the ocean. She sketched the way the light fractured upon the surface, the deep, impenetrable shadows that gathered in the nooks and crannies, the sheer, imposing cliffs that rose like ancient cathedrals of stone, their faces etched with the passage of countless storms. Her early sketches were attempts to capture the raw, physical elements –

the power of the waves, the texture of the rock, the vastness of the sky. But as she spent more time in the cove, a subtle shift began to occur in her work.

The figures Maeve had described began to manifest on her pages. Not literal, drawn figures, but suggestions, impressions. A swirl of water would hint at the sweep of a tail, a pattern of foam on a rock would suggest the curve of a shoulder, the shadow beneath an overhang would morph into the suggestion of a waiting face. It was as if the cove itself was communicating with her, revealing its secrets through the language of form and shadow. She felt a profound connection to this place, a sense of belonging that transcended the ephemeral nature of her visit. It was as if the very essence of the cove recognized a kindred spirit in her, a fellow artist drawn to the elemental forces of the world.

The villagers, however, observed her growing obsession with a mixture of curiosity and apprehension. They saw her, this young American woman, lingering at the water's edge long after the sun had begun its descent, her gaze fixed on the churning currents, her hand moving with an almost feverish intensity across her sketchbook. They saw her disregard for the subtle, yet persistent, warnings they offered – the hushed tones, the averted gazes, the pointed references to the sea's unforgiving nature. For them, Gladys's fascination was not merely artistic curiosity; it was a dangerous flirtation with forces they understood intimately, forces that demanded respect, not artistic interpretation.

Liam, leaning against the bar of his pub, would watch her from a distance when she occasionally ventured back into the village for supplies or a solitary pint. He saw the intensity in her eyes, the way she seemed both lost and found in her art. He appreciated her genuine interest in their home, the way she listened with such rapt attention when he or Maeve spoke of local matters. But there was an edge to her fascination, a recklessness that unsettled him. He had seen what the sea could do, had witnessed its power firsthand, and he recognised the subtle arrogance of someone who believed they could simply capture its essence without truly understanding its heart. "She's drawn to it, that one," he'd murmured to Maeve one evening, his gaze following Gladys as she walked towards the coast road, her sketchbook tucked protectively under her arm. "Like a moth to a flame, and that cove… it's a hungry flame."

Maeve, her eyes, as always, holding a distant, knowing gleam, nodded slowly. "The Cailleach's children are drawn to those who are drawn to her domain," she'd said, her voice soft but carrying a weight of ancient knowledge. "She sees a kindred spirit in the girl, perhaps. But the sea does not give its secrets lightly. And it never forgets." The superstitious villagers, their lives so intimately intertwined with the ebb and flow of the ocean, saw Gladys's prolonged visits to Cailleach's Embrace as a transgression. They saw her sketching the very waters that had claimed so many, her artistic eye dissecting the very elements that held such fearsome power over their lives. They spoke of her in hushed tones, their conversations punctuated by worried glances towards the sea. Was she inviting something? Was she disturbing something best left undisturbed? The folklore, they believed, was not merely superstition; it was a map of the dangers that lurked just beneath the surface of their seemingly tranquil existence.

Gladys, however, remained blissfully, or perhaps perilously, unaware of the growing unease her presence stirred. The world she had left behind – the demanding deadlines, the superficial social circles, the pervasive sense of artistic stagnation – had faded into a distant, hazy memory. Here, in this rugged corner of the world, she had found a visceral connection, a raw inspiration that fueled her creative spirit like never before. She was not seeking danger; she was seeking truth, beauty, and a deeper understanding of herself and the world around her. And she believed, with a fervent artist's conviction, that she had found it in the swirling, hypnotic depths of Cailleach's Embrace. Her sketches were more than just charcoal on paper; they were attempts to translate the ineffable, to capture the spirit of a place that seemed to hold the very essence of ancient power and melancholic beauty. She felt herself becoming a part of the cove's story, a silent observer who, with each stroke of her charcoal, was weaving herself into its narrative, unaware that the story might be far more dangerous than she could ever imagine. The sheer cliffs, the crashing waves, the wind that seemed to whisper secrets – they were her world now, her muse, her sanctuary. She was falling, not into a tragic fate, but into a profound artistic awakening, a journey into the heart of inspiration, where the lines between reality and myth blurred into a captivating, and perhaps perilous, new vision. Her focus was absolute, her immersion complete, and in that complete immersion, lay the seeds of a destiny she could not yet comprehend.

The days bled into one another, marked not by the ticking of a clock, but by the rhythm of the tides and the shifting patterns of light across the water. Gladys became a familiar, if enigmatic, figure to the few hardy souls who still ventured near the cove. They saw her descend the winding, precarious path, a solitary silhouette against the dramatic backdrop of the cliffs. They saw her settle into her chosen spot, her posture one of unwavering focus, her artistic tools laid out with a practiced familiarity. They noted the intensity of her gaze, the way she seemed to be communing with the very elements, drawing something vital from the raw, untamed power of the place.

One afternoon, Liam the pub owner, while checking on a small fishing boat pulled ashore near the cove's less treacherous approach, saw Gladys sketching intently. He'd been told by his wife that Gladys had mentioned wanting to capture the "spirit" of the place, a phrase that had set her teeth on edge. He'd seen enough tourists come and go, their fleeting fascination with the wild beauty of the coast quickly extinguished by the reality of its harshness. But Gladys was different. There was a hunger in her eyes, a depth of engagement that spoke of something more than mere curiosity. As he watched her, he noticed her sketching not just the landscape, but something within it, something that seemed to shimmer just beyond the edges of plain sight. Her hand moved with a frantic energy, her brow furrowed in concentration. She was completely absorbed, oblivious to the gathering clouds or the subtle shift in the wind, which was beginning to carry the first hint of a coming storm.

He hesitated, a battle raging within him. His ingrained sense of caution, honed by years of living in a place where the sea's temper could change in an instant, warred with a growing sense of unease. He'd seen that look before, on the faces of men who'd spent too long staring into the abyss, who'd become too captivated by the siren call of the deep. He considered calling out to her, a friendly word of caution, a reminder of the rapidly changing weather. But he remembered Maeve's words: "The Cailleach's children are drawn to those who are drawn to her domain." There was a destiny at play here, he felt, a force that perhaps even he, with all his local knowledge, could not easily alter. He decided instead to simply watch, a silent, concerned observer on the periphery of her intense communion with the cove.

Further along the coastline, Finn, the taciturn fisherman, was also aware of Gladys's presence. He'd seen her from his boat, a small, solitary figure against the vast expanse of the sea. He'd noticed her persistence, her regular visits to Cailleach's Embrace, a place even many of the local fishermen avoided when the tides were running strong. Finn was a man of the sea, a man who understood its moods, its power, and its secrets. He didn't believe in mermaids or selkies, not in the literal sense, but he understood the primal forces that shaped the coastline, the currents that could drag a man down in seconds, the hidden rocks that could rip the hull of a boat. He saw Gladys's artistic exploration not as a flirtation with myth, but as a dangerous underestimation of the raw, physical power of the ocean. He saw her absorbed in her sketches, her back to the sea, and a silent, almost imperceptible frown would cross his weather-beaten face. He knew the currents around Cailleach's Embrace were particularly vicious, swirling and unpredictable, capable of creating deadly eddies. He'd seen debris, logs, even the occasional unfortunate seabird, disappear into the churning water as if swallowed whole.

One blustery afternoon, as the waves began to churn with a more menacing intensity, Finn was mending his nets on the shore, not far from the path that led down to the cove. He saw Gladys emerging from the mist, her easel and sketchpad secured. She was heading towards the cove, her gait steady, her focus unwavering, despite the increasing strength of the wind that tugged at her hair and whipped her scarf around her face. He watched her descend, a small, determined figure against the grandeur of the darkening sky. He knew that the tide was turning, that the sea would soon be at its most powerful, its most capricious. He continued his work, his movements slow and deliberate, his mind a mixture of professional assessment of the weather and a quiet, almost inarticulate concern for the foreign woman who seemed so captivated by the very forces that commanded his respect and caution. He didn't call out. He never called out. But his gaze lingered on the spot where she disappeared down the path, a silent testament to his awareness of her presence and the unspoken danger that lay ahead. The cove, he knew, had a way of keeping its secrets, and it guarded them fiercely.

First Encounters

Liam watched Gladys from the shadowed interior of his pub, a familiar ache settling in his chest. She was a splash of colour against the muted palette of the Irish coast – the bright scarf tied around her neck, the confident stride that spoke of an American ease he rarely saw in his own countrymen, let alone outsiders drawn to this rugged edge of the world. He'd seen her before, of course. She was becoming a fixture, a solitary silhouette against the brooding sky, her easel a defiant splash of modernity against the ancient rocks. His wife, Eleanor, had mentioned Gladys's fascination, her talk of capturing the 'spirit' of the place. Liam had nodded, a wry smile playing on his lips, while Eleanor had just sighed, a familiar exasperation colouring her tone. "She doesn't understand, Liam," she'd said, her voice soft but firm. "This isn't a postcard. It's alive. And it has teeth."

He understood Eleanor's concern. He'd spent his life on this coastline, had seen its moods shift from gentle caresses to brutal furies in the span of an hour. He'd witnessed the sea claim boats, belongings, and, far too often, lives. He'd learned, through hard-won experience and the quiet wisdom of generations, that the ocean demanded respect, not just admiration. It was a force of nature, ancient and capricious, and those who treated it lightly often paid the highest price. Gladys, with her art supplies and her bright, curious eyes, seemed to embody that very lightness. He'd seen that same look in the eyes of others before her, tourists who'd come seeking a romanticized version of Ireland, only to find themselves humbled, or worse, broken by its reality. There was a hunger in her gaze, though, a depth of engagement that set her apart. It wasn't the fleeting curiosity of a holidaymaker; it was a deliberate seeking, a deep dive into the heart of something.

He remembered an afternoon, just a few days prior, when she'd been sketching near the tide pools. He'd been down by the water's edge, checking on a small fishing boat that had been pulled ashore for repairs, its hull showing the scars of a recent rough crossing. She'd been engrossed, her back to the water, her hand a blur of motion across the page. He'd watched her for a moment, noticing how the wind tugged at her hair, how her scarf fluttered like a captured bird. He'd seen her sketch not just the rocks, the water, the sky, but something else, something almost imperceptible, a shimmer, a distortion in the air just above the water's surface. It was the kind of thing you saw out of the corner of your eye, the trick of light and shadow that the sea played on the unwary. But Gladys seemed to be capturing it, translating it onto her paper with a desperate, almost frantic energy. Her brow was furrowed, her concentration absolute. She was oblivious to the gathering clouds, to the subtle shift in the wind that carried the first hint of a coming storm.

A familiar unease had coiled in his gut. He'd started to walk towards her, his boots crunching on the pebbles, intending to offer a word of caution, a reminder of the rapidly changing weather. But then he'd remembered Maeve's words, spoken just the night before over a pint in his own pub. Maeve, the village's unofficial archivist of local lore, a woman whose eyes seemed to hold the secrets of centuries, had been talking about the cove. "It's the Cailleach's domain, Liam," she'd said, her voice low and resonant, the embers of the peat fire casting dancing shadows across her lined face. "And her children… they are drawn to those who are drawn to her. The girl, she's not just looking at the sea. She's looking *into* it. She's seeing what it wants her to see." Liam had dismissed it then as the usual folklore, the romanticized tales of a woman who lived more in the past than the present. But now, watching Gladys, seeing that same, almost feverish intensity in her work, he felt a prickle of unease. Maeve's words echoed in his mind: *She's seeing what it wants her to see.*

He'd stopped, his feet rooted to the spot. He hadn't called out. What could he say? That the sea was a dangerous mistress? She seemed to know that, in her own way. Perhaps Maeve was right. Perhaps there was a destiny at play, a force that even he, with all his local knowledge, could not easily alter. He'd turned back to his boat, his gaze lingering on Gladys's solitary figure, a silent, concerned observer on the periphery of her intense communion with the cove. He'd seen that look before, on the faces of men who'd spent too long staring into the abyss, who'd become too captivated by the siren call of the deep. He could only hope that Gladys's fascination wouldn't lead her down a path from which there was no return.

Later that week, the opportunity arose for a more direct conversation. Gladys had returned to the village, seeking provisions. She'd come into Liam's pub, a place that served as the social heart of their small community. The air inside was thick with the comforting aroma of peat smoke and stale ale, the low murmur of conversation a constant hum. She looked a little windblown, her cheeks flushed, her eyes bright with an inner fire. She ordered a pint of Guinness, her accent distinctly American, a clear counterpoint to the soft Irish lilt of the locals.

"It's a beautiful, wild place, your coast," she'd said to Liam, her voice carrying easily over the din. She gestured vaguely towards the window, where the grey expanse of the Atlantic was visible in the distance.

Liam wiped down the counter, his movements slow and deliberate. He'd learned to choose his words carefully with outsiders, especially those who seemed to be looking for something more than just a pint and a pleasant chat. "It has its moments," he'd replied, his gaze steady. "But it demands respect, the sea does. It's not to be trifled with."

Gladys had smiled, a genuine, open expression that disarmed him slightly. "Oh, I understand that," she'd said. "But it's also incredibly inspiring. I've never felt such a connection to a place. It's as if it's… speaking to me."

Liam had set down the cloth, leaning on the counter. "Speaking to you, is it?" he'd asked, his tone neutral, but his eyes sharp. "And what is it saying?"

She'd hesitated for a moment, her brow furrowing slightly, as if trying to translate the whispers of the wind into words. "It's… it's telling stories," she'd finally said. "About its past, about the people who lived here, about the power that's always been here. It's in the way the waves crash, in the patterns of the foam, in the very air you breathe. I'm trying to capture that in my art."

He'd nodded slowly, his mind drifting back to Maeve's pronouncements, to the unsettling feeling he'd had watching Gladys sketch. "The sea has a long memory," he'd said, his voice barely above a murmur. "And some memories are best left undisturbed. The cove you favour, Cailleach's Embrace… it has a name that's not given lightly."

A flicker of curiosity, perhaps even a hint of amusement, had crossed Gladys's face. "Maeve told me about the legends," she'd admitted. "The Cailleach, the sea spirits… it's all fascinating. But I'm an artist, not a believer in ghosts."

"Belief has little to do with it," Liam had said, his voice hardening almost imperceptibly. "The currents there are treacherous. They've claimed more than a few souls over the years. People who knew the sea better than any of us." He'd met her gaze directly. "Don't let the beauty blind you to the danger, lass. The sea doesn't care about art. It only cares about survival."

She'd held his gaze for a moment, a hint of defiance in her eyes, but also a flicker of something else, a shadow of doubt perhaps, quickly masked by a confident smile. "I'll be careful, Liam," she'd assured him, picking up her pint. "Thank you for the warning. But I think I'll keep listening to what the sea has to say."

As she turned to leave, her presence a vibrant echo in the quiet pub, Liam had watched her go, a knot of apprehension tightening in his stomach. He knew that the old stories, the folklore that Maeve so readily shared, weren't just fanciful tales. They were warnings, woven into the fabric of the land and sea, passed down through generations for a reason. And Gladys, with her insatiable artistic drive, seemed determined to unravel them, heedless of the potential cost.

Later that same day, as the afternoon sun began its slow descent, casting long shadows across the rugged landscape, Liam saw Finn, the fisherman, making his way back to shore. Finn was a man of few words, his life dictated by the rhythms of the sea, his face a testament to years spent battling the elements. He navigated the coastline in his small, sturdy boat with an expertise that bordered on the innate. Liam had seen him earlier, out on the water, his boat a small, solitary speck against the vast expanse of the Atlantic. Finn was known for his quiet resilience, his almost preternatural understanding of the ocean's moods. He didn't indulge in fanciful notions of mermaids or sea spirits, but he understood the raw, physical power of the water, the currents that could drag a man down in seconds, the hidden rocks that could tear the hull of a boat to shreds.

Liam watched as Finn expertly guided his boat towards a small, sheltered cove, a little further down the coast from Cailleach's Embrace. He saw Finn pull the boat ashore, securing it with practiced ease. The fisherman then began mending his nets on the pebbled beach, his movements slow and deliberate, his weathered hands working with an efficiency born of long habit. Liam, still leaning against the pub door, felt a strange kinship with Finn. They were both men who understood the sea's true nature, who respected its power and its dangers.

He observed Finn as he worked, noticing the slight frown that creased his brow as he glanced towards the general direction of Cailleach's Embrace. It was a subtle gesture, almost imperceptible, but Liam recognized it. It was the look of a man who saw something amiss, who sensed a disturbance in the natural order. Finn had undoubtedly seen Gladys at the cove, her solitary figure a stark contrast to the wild, untamed beauty of the place. Liam imagined Finn's thoughts – the quiet disapproval of an outsider who, in his estimation, was dangerously underestimating the ocean's fury. Finn knew the currents around Cailleach's Embrace were particularly vicious, capable of creating deadly eddies that could swallow a man whole. He'd spoken of it once, years ago, after a particularly brutal storm, describing how debris, even the occasional unfortunate seabird, would simply disappear into the churning water as if claimed by an unseen force.

Liam raised a hand in a casual wave, a gesture Finn acknowledged with a brief nod before returning his attention to his nets. There was no need for words between them. They understood each other through shared experience, through the silent language of those who lived and worked at the mercy of the sea. Liam knew Finn would have seen Gladys heading towards the cove, her easel and sketchpad secured, her gait steady, her focus unwavering, despite the increasing strength of the wind that tugged at her hair and whipped her scarf around her face. He knew Finn would have seen her descend the path, a small, determined figure against the grandeur of the darkening sky. And he knew, as Liam himself knew, that the tide was turning, that the sea would soon be at its most powerful, its most capricious. Finn, Liam surmised, would have felt that same silent, almost inarticulate concern for the foreign woman who seemed so captivated by the very forces that commanded his respect and caution. Finn, like Liam, didn't call out. He never called out. But his gaze, Liam suspected, would have lingered on the spot where Gladys disappeared down the path, a silent testament to his awareness of her presence and the unspoken danger that lay ahead. The cove, Liam knew, had a way of keeping its secrets, and it guarded them fiercely.

The encounter with Liam, while seemingly a polite exchange, had left Gladys with a lingering sense of unease. His words, though delivered with a gruff practicality, carried an undertone of genuine warning that she couldn't entirely dismiss. She'd brushed it off as the typical local caution, the ingrained fear of the sea that permeated their lives. But there was a gravity in his eyes, a depth of experience that suggested his words held more weight than mere superstition. He'd spoken of the sea's long memory, of its desire to keep certain memories undisturbed. He'd mentioned Cailleach's Embrace by name, and the way he said it, the slight hardening of his tone, had caught her attention.

Later that week, seeking a different perspective, Gladys decided to visit Maeve. The old woman lived in a small, stone cottage perched precariously on the hillside overlooking the village. It was a place that seemed to have grown organically from the earth, its walls covered in ivy, its chimney perpetually exhaling a thin curl of smoke. The air around the cottage was thick with the scent of drying herbs and something else, something ancient and earthy that Gladys couldn't quite place. She found Maeve sitting by her hearth, her gnarled hands busy with some intricate mending, her eyes, the colour of faded sea-glass, fixed on the flickering flames.

"Maeve?" Gladys called out softly, stepping into the dim interior.

The old woman looked up, her gaze sharp and unnervingly direct. A slow smile spread across her face, crinkling the corners of her eyes. "Ah, the artist," she said, her voice like the rustle of dry leaves. "I thought I might see you. Liam tells me you're determined to hear the sea's secrets."

Gladys smiled, feeling a strange sense of ease in the old woman's presence, despite the unsettling intensity of her stare. "He warned me," she admitted, settling onto a worn wooden stool. "He said the sea demands respect."

Maeve chuckled, a dry, rasping sound. "Liam is a good man. He knows the sea's moods. But there are other things at play here, child, things older than Liam, older than this village, older than even the stones beneath our feet." She gestured to the seat opposite her. "Sit. Tell me, what is it you see in Cailleach's Embrace? What is it that draws you there with such a hunger?"

Gladys hesitated, searching for the words to articulate the ineffable. "It's… it's the raw power," she began, her voice gaining confidence as she spoke. "The way the light changes, the sheer energy of it all. It feels… ancient. And there are shapes, Maeve, suggestions. In the water, in the rocks. Sometimes, I feel like I'm seeing things, but they're not quite there. Like echoes of something."

Maeve nodded, her expression thoughtful. "Echoes," she repeated softly. "Aye, that's a fitting word. The Cailleach, she was a goddess of winter, of the sea, of storms. They say she carved these shores with her fingernails, that her tears formed the hidden coves and treacherous currents. And they say, on certain nights, when the moon is hidden and the tide is high, that she still walks the shoreline, her cloak woven from sea mist, her voice the roar of the waves."

Gladys listened, captivated. This was the kind of folklore that fuelled her imagination, the raw material from which she drew her inspiration. "And the sacrifices?" she asked, recalling snippets of conversations she'd overheard in the village. "I've heard whispers…"

Maeve's gaze sharpened, and a shadow seemed to pass across her face. "The sea demands a toll," she said, her voice dropping to a near whisper. "Always has. To appease the currents, to ensure safe passage, to placate the ancient powers that reside beneath the waves. There were times, long ago, when offerings were made. Not of blood, perhaps not always. But of devotion. Of commitment. The sea demands a piece of you, child, if you linger too long in its embrace."

"A piece of me?" Gladys echoed, a shiver tracing its way down her spine, not entirely unpleasant. It felt like stepping into a story, a world where myth and reality intertwined.

"Your attention, your focus, your very essence," Maeve clarified. "The sea is a jealous lover. It does not share well. It wants you all to itself. And if you give yourself to it, truly give yourself, it will hold you. Forever." She looked directly at

Gladys, her sea-glass eyes piercing. "You feel it, don't you? The pull. The longing. It's not just the beauty that calls to you. It's something deeper. Something ancient."

Gladys nodded slowly, unable to deny the truth in Maeve's words. She did feel it. A profound connection, a sense of belonging that she had never experienced before. It was more than just artistic inspiration; it was a visceral pull, a feeling of being seen, of being understood by this wild, elemental place.

"You sketch the water's surface," Maeve continued, her gaze drifting towards the window, towards the distant, glittering sea. "But the real stories, the ancient ones, they lie in the depths. And sometimes, the depths reach back." She picked up a smooth, grey stone from the hearth, turning it over in her hands. "This cove," she said, her voice barely audible, "it's a place of powerful currents. And powerful memories. Be careful, Gladys Burton. The sea remembers those who forget their place."

Leaving Maeve's cottage, the old woman's words resonated in Gladys's mind like the echo of a bell. Liam's warning about respect, Maeve's tales of sacrifice and ancient powers – they were not just folklore; they were fragments of a larger truth, a warning that she was venturing into territory far more complex and perhaps far more dangerous than she had initially realised. Yet, instead of deterring her, these cryptic pronouncements only deepened her fascination. The mystery of the cove, the enigmatic nature of its legends, the quiet intensity of the people who lived by its shores – it was all becoming a rich tapestry, a narrative she was increasingly eager to explore, to understand, and ultimately, to capture in her art. She felt as though she was on the cusp of a profound discovery, a revelation that lay hidden just beneath the surface of the churning, enigmatic sea. The call of Cailleach's Embrace was growing stronger, a siren's song promising both inspiration and, perhaps, a truth she was not yet prepared to fully comprehend.

A Preoccupation with the Past

Gladys's sketchpad was no longer a mere collection of observations; it had become a repository of whispered histories, a canvas where the present bled into the past with increasing frequency. She spent hours poring over brittle, yellowed pages salvaged from the small village library, her fingers tracing the faded ink of local chronicles and genealogical records. Her initial fascination with the dramatic sweep of the coastline had subtly, yet undeniably, morphed into a deep-seated preoccupation with its past. The rugged beauty that had initially drawn her in now served as a backdrop, a stage upon which the spectral players of yesteryear were beginning to take center stage. She found herself less interested in the perfect rendering of light on water and more consumed by the stories the water itself seemed to hold.

Her journal entries, once filled with meticulous notes on color palettes and brushstroke techniques, were now a torrent of unearthed legends and tantalizing fragments of local lore. She'd meticulously documented a recurring tale, one that surfaced in multiple disparate accounts, about a woman named Aisling, lost to the sea nearly three centuries ago. The stories were varied in their details, as is the nature of folklore, but a common thread persisted: Aisling had been a woman of remarkable beauty and an almost unnerving connection to the ocean, a kinship that ultimately proved her undoing. Some accounts spoke of her singing to the waves, others of her walking along the tide line even in the fiercest storms, her laughter swallowed by the wind. There were whispers of a betrayal, of a love lost, and of a final, desperate plea to the sea before she was claimed by its unforgiving embrace. Gladys found herself drawn to Aisling with an intensity that bordered on obsession, trying to piece together the shattered remnants of her life, to understand what had compelled her to defy the very element that would become her tomb.

This deep dive into the past was not simply an intellectual pursuit; it was beginning to infuse her art, transforming her creative process. The vibrant, sun-drenched landscapes were giving way to something darker, more introspective. Her sketches of Cailleach's Embrace, once focused on the interplay of light and shadow on the ancient rocks, now featured more pronounced renderings of the churning water, its depths depicted with a brooding intensity. She began to imbue the waves with a semblance of consciousness, sketching them as grasping hands, as spectral faces contorted in eternal lament. The very air around her figures, when she included them, seemed to shimmer with an unseen energy, a palpable tension that hinted at presences just beyond the veil of visibility.

One afternoon, she found herself captivated by a series of rough, charcoal sketches she'd made of a particular rock formation near the cove. The rocks, eroded by centuries of salt spray and relentless waves, had been shaped into formations that, with a little imagination, resembled hunched figures. Gladys had initially sketched them simply as an interesting geological feature. But now, looking back at the smudged lines and darkened shadows, she saw not mere rock, but the silent guardians of ancient secrets, their stony faces turned perpetually towards the turbulent sea, their postures suggesting an unending vigil. She began to add subtle details – a suggestion of flowing hair in the spray, a vacant stare in the shadowed hollows of the stone – transforming the natural into the supernatural.

She also felt an increasing disconnect from the present. Conversations in the village, once a source of colour and human interaction, now seemed to her like distant echoes, their concerns trivial compared to the grand narratives she was uncovering. Liam's pragmatic warnings about the sea's dangers, while still acknowledged, felt like cautionary tales aimed at a different kind of visitor, one less attuned to the deeper currents of history and myth. Even Maeve's pronouncements, which had initially felt so profound, now seemed to Gladys like mere footnotes to a much larger, more complex story that she was only beginning to decipher. She found herself retreating, seeking solace and inspiration not in human company, but in the solitary communion with the past, with the ghosts that haunted the coastline.

Her isolation was further amplified by the physical toll her obsession was taking. She was spending longer hours at the cove, often until dusk began to settle, the relentless wind and the encroaching chill barely registering. Her diet consisted of whatever she could grab quickly – a piece of bread, an apple – sustenance taken not for pleasure, but purely to fuel her relentless pursuit. Sleep became a luxury, often interrupted by vivid dreams filled with the roar of waves and the mournful cries of seabirds, dreams that felt more like memories than mere figments of her imagination. Her art, once a source of joy and release, had become an imperative, a desperate attempt to capture fleeting visions and half-heard whispers before they dissolved into the vastness of the ocean.

The journal entries became more fragmented, more impassioned. "The sea doesn't just reflect the sky," she scrawled one evening, her handwriting jagged and urgent. "It remembers. It holds everything. Aisling wasn't lost; she was taken. Claimed. Her spirit is still here, I can feel it. It's in the way the water pulls at the pebbles, the way the light catches the foam. It's not just the landscape I'm painting, it's the memory of a life, the echoes of a soul." Another entry read: "Liam says I'm being foolish, chasing shadows. But he doesn't understand. This isn't about chasing. It's about being found. The sea has found me. Aisling has found me."

She began to experiment with new mediums, incorporating sand and sea salt into her paints, attempting to give her canvases a tangible connection to the environment. Her palette shifted towards muted blues, greys, and greens, punctuated by the stark white of crashing foam and the deep, unsettling black of the ocean's abyssal depths. Her figures, when they appeared, were often indistinct, mere suggestions of form emerging from the elemental chaos of the sea. She was no longer just an observer; she was becoming a conduit, a translator of the ancient, enduring language of the ocean and its lost inhabitants. The intensity of her focus was palpable, a solitary flame burning against the encroaching darkness, driven by a thirst for a past that refused to remain buried. The beauty of the place was no longer enough; she needed its secrets, its sorrows, its enduring power, and she was willing to delve into its darkest depths to find them.

The Eve of Disappearance

The air in 'The Salty Dog' pub was thick with the scent of stale ale, brine, and the underlying earthiness of peat smoke. It was a familiar perfume to Gladys, one that usually settled her nerves, but tonight, it only seemed to amplify the buzzing beneath her skin. The low murmur of conversations, the clatter of pewter mugs, the occasional burst of laughter – it all felt distant, like sounds heard through a dense fog. She nursed a lukewarm cider, her gaze flitting between the familiar faces clustered around the rough-hewn tables and the darkening rectangle of the pub's window, where the last vestiges of twilight clung to the sky.

She had come, ostensibly, for the camaraderie, a last chance to feel connected to the rhythm of the village before… before what, she couldn't quite articulate, even to herself. The past few weeks had been an immersion, a descent into a world that felt both ancient and terrifyingly present. Aisling's story, or rather the fragmented whispers of it, had woven themselves into the very fabric of Gladys's being. The salt-laced wind that whipped around the coastline seemed to carry Aisling's sighs, the relentless crash of waves against the shore echoed a sorrow that transcended centuries. Her sketchpad, now a repository of frantic charcoal lines and washes of ink that mirrored the turbulent sea, felt less like a collection of observations and more like an artifact unearthed from a forgotten time. She had found herself sketching the very essence of longing, of a yearning so profound it could draw a soul into the depths.

Maeve, her face etched with the wisdom of seasons and stories, approached her table, her movements as fluid and graceful as the tide Gladys had come to know so intimately. Maeve's eyes, the colour of a stormy sea, held a knowing glint. "Lost in thought, lass?" she asked, her voice a low, comforting rumble.

Gladys startled, then offered a strained smile. "Just… thinking about the light, Maeve. It changes so quickly this time of year." It was a half-truth. The light, yes, but also the shadows it cast, the hidden depths it concealed.

Maeve chuckled, a sound like pebbles rolling in the surf. "The light always changes, Gladys. It's the darkness that holds the secrets." She sat down, her gaze falling upon Gladys's open sketchpad, which Gladys had instinctively tried to shield. Maeve's fingers, gnarled but surprisingly nimble, reached out, tracing the jagged lines of a drawing that depicted the Cailleach's Embrace rocks, their forms twisted and imbued with a life Gladys had only recently discovered. The spray from the sea, rendered in bold, sweeping strokes, seemed to coil around them like spectral arms.

"You see it now, don't you?" Maeve murmured, her voice barely audible above the pub's din. "The truth beneath the surface."

Gladys's heart hammered against her ribs. Maeve's words resonated with a chilling accuracy. She had felt a breakthrough, a dawning comprehension that had eclipsed all her previous efforts. The sketches were no longer just representations; they were emanations, tangible links to the spectral narratives she was uncovering. "It's… it's more than I imagined," Gladys confessed, her voice hushed, her eyes wide with a peculiar blend of exhilaration and dread. She wanted to explain the feeling, the almost tangible presence she'd sensed while sketching the ancient rocks, the way the very air seemed to thrum with an ancient power, but the words felt inadequate, too fragile to contain the immensity of her discovery. She felt a profound connection to Aisling, a kinship that transcended the centuries, a shared understanding of a beauty so potent it verged on dangerous.

"There are stories, Gladys," Maeve continued, her gaze fixed on a particularly dark swirl of ink, "that the sea doesn't just take. It calls. And sometimes, those who are most attuned to its song… they answer."

Gladys nodded, unable to speak, a shiver tracing its way down her spine despite the warmth of the pub. She felt as if Maeve was looking not at her sketches, but into her very soul, seeing the obsession that had taken root and blossomed with alarming speed. Her artistic process had become a ritual, a desperate attempt to decipher the ocean's ancient dialect, to translate its grief and its longing into lines and colours. The muted palettes of blues, greys, and greens, punctuated by the stark white of foam and the profound black of the deep, were not mere artistic choices; they were the colours of memory, of loss, of a beauty that had been irrevocably intertwined with tragedy.

Liam, from his usual corner perch, watched the interaction with a growing unease. Gladys's intensity, her retreat from the ordinary world into the enigmatic depths of the past, had been a constant source of quiet concern. He saw the flush on her cheeks, the way her eyes darted towards the window, a restless energy radiating from her. He had tried, in his own quiet way, to ground her, to remind her of the tangible realities of their lives, the predictable cycle of tides and seasons, the solid earth beneath their feet. But lately, his words seemed to bounce off her, absorbed by some internal vortex that pulled her further and further from him, from everyone.

His gaze shifted to Finn, who had joined Maeve and Gladys at their table. Finn, the taciturn fisherman, his face a map of weathered lines, his eyes the colour of the deep ocean on a starless night. Finn rarely spoke, but when he did, his words carried the weight of unspoken knowledge, of a life lived in constant communion with the sea's raw power. Liam observed the subtle shift in Finn's posture as he leaned closer to Gladys, his gaze steady and unreadable. Gladys, in turn, seemed to lean into Finn's presence, her earlier agitation giving way to a focused intensity as she spoke to him, her hands gesturing animatedly as she pointed to her sketchpad. Whatever they were discussing, it was clearly significant, a shared confidence that excluded everyone else, including Liam. There was an unspoken understanding between them, a tacit acknowledgment of a conversation that existed on a plane he couldn't access. Finn's expression was a perfect, unnerving blank slate, revealing nothing, yet implying everything. Liam felt a prickle of something akin to jealousy, but it was overshadowed by a more pervasive, primal fear. He saw in Finn a reflection of the sea itself – ancient, powerful, and utterly inscrutable.

Maeve, sensing Liam's unease, gave him a subtle, almost imperceptible nod, a silent acknowledgment of his disquiet. She understood the currents that ran beneath the surface of their small community, the unspoken histories that bound them together, and sometimes, tore them apart. She had seen this kind of fascination before, this intoxicating pull towards the ancient and the unknown, and she knew it could be both a blessing and a curse.

Gladys, oblivious to Liam's disquiet and Maeve's subtle communication, turned back to her sketchpad, her eyes alight with a fierce, almost feverish excitement. She was close, she felt it. The fragmented whispers, the tantalizing glimpses into Aisling's life – they were coalescing, forming a narrative that felt both inevitable and profoundly personal. She wanted to capture this moment, this clarity, before it slipped away. "I think," she began, her voice trembling slightly, "I've found it. The place. The moment."

Finn's response was a low, almost guttural sound, a murmur that seemed to be swallowed by the pub's ambient noise, but Gladys understood. He understood. He had seen her drawings, he had heard her talk, and he had recognized the truth in her artistic revelations. There was a shared language between them, one that bypassed words and spoke directly to the soul.

Liam's unease solidified into a cold knot of dread. He had never been comfortable with Finn's silent intensity, his uncanny ability to navigate the sea in conditions that would send others to the shore. There was a wildness in Finn, a primal connection to the elements that Liam, grounded in the practicalities of his own life, found both fascinating and terrifying. He watched as Gladys began to pack away her sketchpad, her movements sharp and decisive. The conversation had clearly reached its conclusion, and the air around her felt charged with a new purpose.

As the evening drew to a close, and the patrons began to drift out into the cool night air, Gladys made her announcement, her voice clear and ringing with a newfound conviction. "I'm going to the cove at dawn," she declared, her gaze sweeping over the familiar faces. "Just one last time. To capture the light. Before it all... changes."

Liam's breath hitched. Dawn. At the cove. The Cailleach's Embrace. The very place where Aisling's legend was most potent, where the sea's embrace was said to be both a cradle and a tomb. A wave of cold dread washed over him, a premonition as sharp and biting as the sea spray. He knew, with a certainty that chilled him to the bone, that this was not merely an artistic excursion. Gladys was not just seeking inspiration; she was seeking something else entirely. She was walking towards a precipice, drawn by a force she couldn't comprehend, a force that had already claimed so many echoes from this ancient coastline. And as he watched her gather her things, her face illuminated by the flickering lamplight, he felt a profound sense of helplessness, a silent scream trapped in his throat. The siren's call was growing louder, and he feared Gladys was already too far under its spell to turn back. The night was young, but the dawn already held a chilling promise.

CHAPTER TWO — THE TIDE TURNS

The Discovery

The grey dawn had crept in like a thief, stealing the last vestiges of night with a brutal efficiency. Gladys, fueled by an artist's obsession and Maeve's cryptic pronouncements, had slipped out of her small cottage long before the first tentative rays of light had even considered breaching the horizon. Her sketchpad, along with a small bag containing her camera and a thermos of lukewarm tea, were her only companions as she navigated the familiar, yet suddenly menacing, path towards the cove. The air was thick with an oppressive stillness, the usual cacophony of the sea muted, as if holding its breath in anticipation. She had felt it last night, a magnetic pull towards the Cailleach's Embrace, a place where the whispers of the past had become a siren's song, drowning out all other sounds, all other thoughts. The cryptic words Maeve had spoken, about the sea calling and those attuned to its song answering, had replayed in her mind, morphing from unsettling pronouncements into a prophecy she was compelled to fulfill. She clutched her worn camera, its familiar weight a small comfort against the burgeoning unease that coiled in her stomach. The sketches were no longer enough; she needed to see it, to *feel* it, to capture the ephemeral beauty and the raw power that had held her captive for weeks. The treacherous rocks, usually a stark and dramatic silhouette against the sky, were now mere shades of grey in the pre-dawn gloom, their danger amplified by the invisibility. Each step was a deliberate act, a surrender to a force she no longer had the will, or perhaps the desire, to resist. The wind, when it finally stirred, was a cold, mournful sigh that tugged at her coat, as if trying to pull her back from the brink. But Gladys pressed on, her eyes fixed on the indistinct line where the sea met the sky, a horizon that promised both revelation and oblivion.

Back in the village, the rhythm of life began to stir with a reluctant slowness. Liam, his sleep restless and troubled, was the first to notice Gladys's absence. He'd woken with a start, a vague sense of foreboding clinging to him like the damp sea mist. The cottage was silent, the kettle cold, her boots gone from their usual place by the door. He tried to dismiss it, telling himself she'd simply gone for an early walk, a habit she'd fallen into with increasing frequency. But the knot of dread in his stomach tightened with each passing minute. Maeve, too, found herself glancing towards Gladys's cottage, a quiet concern etched on her face. She had seen the fire in Gladys's eyes last night, a dangerous spark that spoke of a singular, all-consuming focus. She knew the allure of the cove, the ancient power that pulsed beneath its surface, and she feared that Gladys, in her desperate quest for understanding, had stepped too close to the edge.

By mid-morning, the unease had begun to ripple through the small community. Gladys was a stranger, an outsider, but she had become a fixture, her quiet intensity a part of the village's fabric. When Maeve's discreet inquiries confirmed she hadn't been seen returning, a quiet panic began to set in. Liam, his face pale and drawn, was already organizing a search party. He felt a desperate urgency, a sickening premonition that his fears were no idle fancy. He'd tried to dissuade her, to anchor her to the solid ground of their present, but she had been lost, adrift in the currents of the past. Now, the sea, that vast, indifferent entity, seemed to have claimed her.

The search began in earnest. Liam, his voice tight with a suppressed panic, directed the small group of villagers who had gathered, their faces etched with concern. They fanned out along the coastline, their calls of "Gladys!" swallowed by the relentless roar of the waves. Finn, his usual stoic demeanor unreadable, joined the search, his knowledge of the coastline, its hidden coves and treacherous currents, invaluable. He moved with a quiet efficiency, his eyes scanning the churning water and the rocky shore with an intensity that spoke volumes. Maeve, too frail for the arduous trek, remained in the village, her fingers tracing the patterns on an old, sea-worn shawl, her prayers whispered against the wind. She knew the sea's moods, its capacity for both beauty and brutality, and her heart ached with a premonition of loss.

The Gardaí were alerted, their presence a stark reminder of the gravity of the situation. Inspector Davies, a man whose pragmatism was as ingrained as the salt in the sea air, arrived with his team, their official vehicles a jarring contrast to the weathered simplicity of the village. He listened patiently to Liam's frantic account, his expression carefully neutral, but his eyes betrayed a flicker of concern. He understood the dangers of the coastline, the unpredictable nature of the Atlantic, and he knew that young women, especially those drawn to solitary pursuits, could easily fall victim to its treacherous embrace. The initial assessment was grim: a tragic accident, a young woman caught unawares by the unforgiving sea.

As the hours ticked by, the search widened, encompassing a larger swathe of the coastline. The tide, which had been out at dawn, was now beginning to turn, its relentless surge an ominous presence. Liam's hope dwindled with each passing minute, replaced by a gnawing despair. He pictured Gladys, her vibrant spirit, her artistic soul, swallowed by the unforgiving depths. He remembered her last words at the pub, her declaration of intent to visit the cove at dawn, her fascination with the light, the shadows, the secrets the sea held. He had felt it then, a premonition of danger, a chilling certainty that she was walking into something far beyond her understanding.

It was late afternoon when Finn, his face impassive, emerged from the spray and mist near the base of the Cailleach's Embrace. He carried something carefully in his arms, a bundle wrapped in an oilskin. The hushed silence that fell over the assembled villagers was absolute, broken only by the crashing of the waves. As Finn approached, the grim reality of what he held became all too apparent. It was Gladys.

Her body, pale and eerily still, lay cradled in Finn's arms. Her clothes, once a vibrant splash of colour against the monochromatic landscape, were now torn and sodden, clinging to her like a second skin. But it was her hand that drew every eye. Clutched with an almost desperate grip was her camera, its lens pointed towards the unforgiving sky, as if she had been trying to capture one last image, one final testament to her artistic vision, even in her final moments. Her hair, usually tied back neatly, was a tangled, seaweed-strewn mess, framing a face that was frozen in a silent scream, or perhaps, a final, startled gasp. There was a faint, dark bruise blooming on her temple, a stark contrast to the pallor of her skin.

Inspector Davies knelt beside her, his movements deliberate and professional, though a flicker of profound sadness crossed his features. He examined her briefly, his gloved fingers gentle as he checked for signs of life, a formality that was painfully obvious. The camera, he noted, was still clutched in her rigid grasp. He spoke quietly to his officers, his voice low and measured, but the words "accidental drowning" and "treacherous currents" were clearly discernible. The notorious danger of the Cailleach's Embrace was no secret; it was a place whispered about in hushed tones, a graveyard of ships and sailors, a testament to the sea's untamed power. The initial assessment was swift, almost too swift, a neat conclusion drawn from a scene that felt… wrong.

Liam, his world collapsing around him, stumbled forward, his throat too tight to utter a sound. He looked at Gladys, his Gladys, the woman who had brought a spark of life and colour into his quiet existence, and saw only a tragic tableau. The camera, he realized with a sickening lurch, was the same one she had been so eager to use, the one she had filled with her visions of the past. Had she finally found what she was looking for? Had her artistic quest led her to this desolate end?

Maeve arrived, supported by a worried neighbour, her eyes wide and fixed on Gladys's still form. She approached slowly, her gaze softening with a profound sorrow. She looked at the camera, at the way Gladys's fingers were curled around it, and a shiver, unrelated to the cold, ran down her spine. It felt… deliberate. As if Gladys had intentionally placed herself there, with her camera, in a final, defiant act. The bruise on her temple, too, seemed more than a mere consequence of a fall; it looked like a mark, a deliberate imprint. The sea was a cruel mistress, Maeve knew, but it rarely staged such perfect, chillingly picturesque scenes. There was a narrative here, a story woven into the very fabric of Gladys's final moments, a narrative that whispered of something more sinister than a simple, tragic accident. The salt-laced wind seemed to carry not just the scent of brine, but the faint, spectral echo of Aisling's sorrow, a sorrow that had now claimed another soul. The tide had indeed turned, not just for Gladys, but for the fragile peace of their isolated world.

Detective O'Connell Arrives

Detective Liam O'Connell's battered navy sedan, a familiar sight in the more rural parts of the country, crunched to a halt on the gravel track overlooking the cove. The air, even inside the sealed car, seemed heavy with the damp, salty breath of the Atlantic, a scent that clung to everything along this unforgiving coastline. O'Connell, a man whose very presence seemed to absorb the muted light of the overcast sky, cut the engine. The sudden silence was profound, broken only by the rhythmic, unceasing sigh of the waves below. He'd been briefed on the train, the sparse details painting a picture of a tragic accident, a young artist, a notorious stretch of coastline. But O'Connell carried with him the weight of too many "accidents" that were anything but. His past investigations had taught him that the most beautiful landscapes often hid the ugliest truths, and this rugged, windswept corner of Ireland felt particularly potent with unspoken history.

He stepped out of the car, the chill seeping through his tweed jacket. The scene below was a tableau of grim efficiency: a handful of local Gardaí, their uniforms stark against the muted greens and greys of the landscape, and the hushed, anxious faces of the villagers gathered a little distance away. Inspector Davies, a man O'Connell had crossed paths with on previous cases, a solid, no-nonsense officer with a weary kindness in his eyes, met him near the cordon.

"O'Connell," Davies greeted, his voice a low rumble, "Nasty business."

O'Connell nodded, his gaze sweeping across the scene. The body, covered by a standard-issue blanket, was still there, a stark, undeniable fact against the wild backdrop. "Tell me what you have, Inspector."

Davies gestured towards the edge of the cliff. "Gladys Quinn, twenty-eight. Artist, moved here about six months ago. Found by a local fisherman, Finn O'Malley, early this afternoon. She'd been out since dawn, apparently. Went to sketch at the Cailleach's Embrace. It's a treacherous spot, as you know."

O'Connell's eyes narrowed, his gaze lingering on the cluster of items carefully arranged near where the body had been discovered, before it was moved. A sketchbook, its pages presumably waterlogged, a thermos, a small bag. They looked… placed. Deliberately so. "Sketchbook, thermos, bag," he murmured, more to himself than Davies. "Anything else?"

"Her camera," Davies said, pointing to a young officer carefully bagging a professional-looking SLR camera, its lens still uncapped. "Found clutched in her hand. Or rather, near her hand. Rigor mortis had set in, making it a bit difficult to ascertain the exact position, but it was certainly in close proximity. We believe she was trying to take a photograph."

O'Connell's brow furrowed. "Clutched in her hand? Or near it?" The subtle distinction was significant. A death grip suggested a struggle, a final desperate act. Proximity might imply something else entirely. He began his own slow circuit of the immediate area, his movements methodical, his eyes absorbing every detail. The rocky outcrop where she'd been found was slick with sea spray, the tide still on its relentless ebb. He noticed the precise way her boots were positioned, almost parallel, a small distance from the edge of the steep descent. Too neat for someone who had lost their footing in a panicked fall.

"She was alone?" O'Connell asked, his gaze fixed on a faint scuff mark on the rock face, barely visible beneath a sheen of salt.

"As far as we know," Davies replied. "There's a local lad, Liam Gallagher, who seems to have been close to her. He's the one who's been most visibly distraught. Says she often went out early for inspiration. He organized a search when she didn't return."

O'Connell knelt, pulling on a pair of latex gloves. He approached the bagged camera, the plastic rustling softly. Davies was right; the camera was remarkably well-preserved, almost as if it had been protected. He peered through the plastic at the lens. What had Gladys Quinn been looking at in her final moments? What had she tried to capture? His mind was already piecing together fragments, forming hypotheses that danced just beyond his immediate grasp. The bruise on her temple, Davies had mentioned it in his preliminary report. Small, he'd said, almost insignificant. But O'Connell knew that the smallest detail could often be the most revealing.

He stood, turning his attention back to the scattered belongings. The sketchbook. If it contained sketches of the Cailleach's Embrace, it could offer insight into her state of mind, her focus. Were the sketches of the place itself, or something within it? He looked out at the vast, indifferent expanse of the sea, its grey waves crashing against the jagged rocks with an almost predatory patience. The locals called this place the Cailleach's Embrace. The 'Hag's Embrace.' A name steeped in folklore and a warning.

"The tide," O'Connell observed, watching the water recede, exposing more of the treacherous, seaweed-slicked rocks. "When did it turn?"

"Low tide was around dawn, maybe a little after," Davies supplied. "She'd have been caught by the incoming tide if she'd fallen in then."

"Or if someone wanted it to look that way," O'Connell added softly, his gaze drifting towards the village nestled in the distance, a cluster of stone cottages against the imposing backdrop of the hills. He'd learned that the sea, while powerful, was also a convenient accomplice, its vastness and unpredictability capable of concealing a multitude of sins.

He walked over to where the body had lain, examining the damp sand. He noted the absence of any significant disturbance beyond what would be expected from the arrival of the first responders. No scattered rocks, no frantic gouges in the earth. It was as if she had simply… settled there. He picked up a small, smooth stone, turning it over in his gloved fingers. The sea was a formidable force, but it also had a peculiar way of washing away evidence, of tidying up the scene.

"The local fisherman, O'Malley," O'Connell said, his eyes scanning the cliff face for any subtle signs of a struggle or a fall that might have been missed. "Did he see anything? Anyone else around?"

"He reported seeing no one else," Davies confirmed. "Said he found her on his usual morning patrol of the fishing grounds. Saw her from a distance, the colour of her clothing against the rocks."

O'Connell continued his slow, deliberate examination of the ground. He noticed a faint, almost imperceptible scuff mark on a boulder near where the camera had been found, higher up the incline than he would expect from a slip near the water's edge. It was small, easily overlooked, but it snagged his attention. It looked like the mark of a shoe, perhaps, made by someone bracing themselves or pushing off. He crouched, examining it closely. It was too precise to be accidental.

"Inspector," O'Connell called, pointing to the mark. "Get forensics to have a look at this. And the area around it."

Davies joined him, squinting at the faint abrasion. "Could be anything, O'Connell. Wind, debris…"

"Or it could be someone standing here," O'Connell countered, his voice calm but firm. He stood, his eyes tracing an invisible line from the scuff mark down towards the water's edge. "Someone who wasn't necessarily watching the waves." He then looked at the positioning of Gladys's belongings again. The thermos, the sketchbook, the bag – all neatly placed, as if she'd set them down before contemplating the view. But her camera, the crucial piece of evidence, was found near her body, almost as if it had been dropped or knocked from her grasp. The contrast was jarring. If she'd set down her belongings to take a photo, wouldn't the camera have been with them? Unless, of course, the camera was the reason she was there, and the other items were merely incidental.

O'Connell decided to speak with Liam Gallagher. He found him by the cordoned-off area, his face etched with a grief that O'Connell recognized all too well. The young man's eyes were red-rimmed, his shoulders slumped. He clutched a damp handkerchief, twisting it nervously in his hands.

"Liam?" O'Connell approached him gently. "I'm Detective O'Connell. I'm taking over the investigation."

Gallagher looked up, his gaze a mixture of desperation and a flicker of hope. "You… you'll find out what happened, won't you?"

"That's my job," O'Connell said, his voice steady. "I need to ask you a few questions about Gladys. When did you last see her?"

"Yesterday evening," Gallagher replied, his voice thick with emotion. "We were at the pub. She was… excited. Talking about coming out here at dawn. She said the light at the Cailleach's Embrace was… special. Magical, she called it." He swallowed hard. "She was always looking for that perfect light, that perfect moment for her art."

"Did she seem worried? Troubled?" O'Connell pressed.

Gallagher hesitated, his brow furrowing. "Not troubled, exactly. More… intense. Like she was on the verge of something. She'd been spending a lot of time in the village archives, looking at old records, old photographs. Said she felt a connection to the history here, a pull." He gestured vaguely towards the sea. "She was fascinated by the stories, the old legends."

"Legends about the Cailleach's Embrace?" O'Connell inquired, his interest piqued.

Gallagher nodded. "The Cailleach herself. A sea spirit, they say. Guarding something. Or waiting for something. And the cove… it's where she's supposed to appear. Gladys was captivated by it all. She felt it was… important for her work." He looked down at the ground. "I tried to tell her it was dangerous. That the sea here is unforgiving."

O'Connell filed this information away. An artist drawn to local folklore, seeking inspiration in a place known for its perilous reputation. It was a narrative that fit the superficial facts, but O'Connell felt the subtle dissonances. The meticulous placement of the belongings, the camera found near her hand but not quite in it, the small scuff mark on the rock. These weren't the hallmarks of a straightforward accident.

He walked back towards the edge of the cliff, gazing down at the water. The sun, a pale disc behind the clouds, cast a watery light on the scene. He noticed a small cluster of rocks, further out than the main body of the cove, that remained exposed even at high tide. It was a lonely, windswept outcrop, accessible only by a perilous scramble across slick, seaweed-covered stones. He wondered if Gladys had gone out there. Had she been trying to capture a more dramatic angle?

He then considered Maeve, the elderly woman Davies had mentioned as being concerned. An artist's intuition often resonated with those who held a deeper understanding of the world, those who lived closer to its primal forces. He would need to speak with her as well. The sea kept its secrets well, but sometimes, if you listened carefully enough, you could hear the whispers of those who had been lost to its depths. And O'Connell was an excellent listener. He had a feeling that Gladys Quinn's story was far from over, and that the tide had indeed turned, not just for her, but for the quiet village and its hidden secrets. The Cailleach's Embrace had claimed a life, but O'Connell was beginning to suspect it had been a willing participant, or perhaps, a victim of something far more deliberate than a rogue wave. His instincts, honed by years of experience, screamed that this was not just a tragic accident. This was a carefully orchestrated tragedy. He looked at the sea again, its ceaseless motion a mesmerizing, yet menacing, spectacle. It held the answers, he was sure of it, buried beneath the salt and the spray. And he was determined to unearth them.

Initial Investigations and Local Suspicions

Detective O'Connell's initial investigations into Gladys Burton's death began not with the dramatic pronouncements of a seasoned city detective, but with the quiet, methodical observation of a man attuned to the subtle rhythms of a close-knit community. The air in the village of Ballyknock, still heavy with the scent of salt and the unspoken grief that hung over the cove, felt dense with a different kind of atmosphere altogether – one of ingrained suspicion. He started at the heart of the village, 'The Salty Siren,' the only pub in miles, a place that served as both a social hub and a repository of local lore. The proprietor, Liam, a man whose weathered face spoke of long hours and early mornings, was the first to be drawn into O'Connell's orbit. Liam, as O'Connell had already gathered, was one of the last people to have seen Gladys alive.

"She was a bright spark, wasn't she?" Liam began, wiping down the counter with a practiced hand, his gaze fixed on the dark, gleaming wood. "Full of life. Always sketching, always looking for something new. That cove, the Cailleach's Embrace, it drew her like a moth to a flame." He paused, his eyes meeting O'Connell's in the dim light of the pub. "Said it had a certain… energy. A raw, untamed beauty that spoke to her soul."

O'Connell nodded, his notebook open. "When did you last speak with her?"

"Yesterday evening," Liam replied, his voice a low rumble, tinged with the local accent. "She was here, like she often was. Had a cup of tea, showed me some of her work. Beautiful stuff, really. Capturing the light on the water, the drama of the cliffs. She seemed… excited. Almost feverish, about going out to the Embrace at dawn. Said she had a feeling, a premonition about the light there that morning." He sighed, the sound a gentle exhalation of sorrow. "I told her it was a fool's errand, going out there alone, especially at that hour. But she just smiled. Said the best art often comes from taking risks."

"Did she mention anyone else? Anyone she was meeting, or anyone she was concerned about?" O'Connell probed, his pen moving across the page.

Liam shook his head. "No, nothing like that. She was a private person, in her own way. Kept herself to herself, mostly. But she was friendly enough. Talked to anyone who'd listen about her art. She'd been spending a lot of time in the old records office, looking through old maps and parish documents, too. Said she was trying to understand the 'essence' of the place, the history woven into the very rocks and the sea." He leaned closer, his voice dropping to a more confidential tone. "Some of the older folk, they don't like outsiders digging into things best left buried. They've got their own ways of looking at the world, and the sea. It's not just water to them, you see."

O'Connell's mind cataloged Liam's words. The 'essence' of the place. The 'history woven into the very rocks.' The unease about outsiders. This was precisely the undercurrent he'd sensed upon his arrival. The community wasn't just grieving; it was also wary.

Leaving the pub, O'Connell made his way to a small, stone cottage nestled on the edge of the village, its windows looking out towards the wild Atlantic. This was the home of Maeve O'Sullivan, a woman whose name had been whispered to him by Inspector Davies as someone who "knew things."

Maeve, a spry woman in her late seventies, with eyes that held the wisdom of generations and a resilience etched into her features, greeted him on her doorstep. Her cottage was a testament to a life lived in close communion with the land and its stories; the scent of peat smoke and dried herbs filled the air.

"Detective O'Connell," Maeve greeted, her voice surprisingly strong for her age. "I heard you were coming. A sad day for Ballyknock."

"Mrs. O'Sullivan," O'Connell began, tipping his hat politely. "Thank you for seeing me. I understand you have a deep knowledge of the local history and folklore."

Maeve gestured for him to enter, her movements precise and deliberate. "I've lived here all my life, Detective. My grandmother before me, and hers before that. We know the land, and we know the sea. And we know the stories the sea tells." She settled herself into a worn armchair by the hearth, a shawl draped over her shoulders. "This cove, the Cailleach's Embrace, it's always been a place of... power. And danger."

"Gladys Quinn was drawn to it," O'Connell stated, sitting opposite her.

Maeve's eyes seemed to look beyond him, towards the distant, turbulent sea. "She was an artist, you said? Artists feel things, don't they? They feel the currents beneath the surface. The Cailleach herself... she's an old spirit. A sea hag, some call her. She guards this stretch of coast, or perhaps, she waits. The stories are old, and they shift like the tides, but they all speak of a possessive nature. She doesn't like to be disturbed, not by those who don't understand."

O'Connell made a mental note. Possessive nature. Disturbance. "Did she speak to you about the cove, Mrs. O'Sullivan?"

"She came by once or twice," Maeve said, her gaze distant. "Asked questions about the old tales. About the women who were lost to the sea here over the centuries. She was fascinated by the tragic stories, the whispers of enchantments, of curses. She seemed to think it was all part of the landscape, part of the 'muse' as she called it." Maeve shook her head slowly. "I warned her. I told her the sea here has a long memory. It takes what it wants, and it doesn't give back easily. Especially not to those who look too closely, who pry into its secrets."

"What kind of secrets?" O'Connell pressed, his focus sharpening.

"The kind that are best left undisturbed, Detective," Maeve replied, her voice firm. "The kind that bind the land to the sea, and the past to the present. There are places where the veil between worlds is thin. The Cailleach's Embrace is one of them. Some believe it's a place where souls can become trapped, lost between the living and the dead. And the Cailleach, she… she doesn't like trespassers."

O'Connell recognized the subtle shift from factual recounting to the realm of superstition, but he also understood that in communities like Ballyknock, superstition often held a kernel of truth, or at least, a reflection of collective anxieties and unacknowledged events. He thanked Maeve for her time, her words echoing in his mind. An artist's fascination with morbid history, a warning from a village elder about an ancient spirit. It was a narrative steeped in the local colour, but O'Connell remained tethered to the tangible evidence.

His next encounter was with Finn O'Malley, the fisherman who had discovered Gladys's body. O'Connell found him mending nets by his small, weather-beaten boat, the 'Sea Serpent,' pulled up on the shingle beach just beyond the village.

Finn was a man of few words, his face a landscape of hard-won experience, his hands calloused and weathered by years of battling the elements. He looked up as O'Connell approached, his expression unreadable, a stoic mask that offered no invitation for easy conversation.

"Mr. O'Malley," O'Connell began, his voice measured. "Detective O'Connell. I need to ask you about what you saw this morning."

Finn nodded curtly, his eyes never leaving the task at hand, the intricate weaving of the net. "Saw what I saw, Detective. A tragedy."

"You found her at the Cailleach's Embrace?"

"Aye." A single word, devoid of emotion.

"Did you see anyone else in the area? Anyone else near the cove when you arrived?" O'Connell watched Finn's hands, the steady, rhythmic movement of his fingers as they worked the twine.

Finn paused for a fraction of a second, then resumed his work. "Was no one else there. Just the sea, and the rocks, and… her."

"And how did you find her?" O'Connell pressed, his gaze unwavering. "Can you describe the scene when you first saw her?"

Finn laid down his net, turning to face O'Connell fully. His eyes, the colour of a stormy sea, held a depth that O'Connell found disquieting. "She was on the rocks. Near the edge. The tide was coming in. I saw her from the boat. Knew it was bad straight away."

"When you say, 'near the edge,' can you be more specific? Was she at the very precipice, or further back?"

Finn hesitated, his jaw clenching almost imperceptibly. "She was… down a bit. On a ledge. Not where you'd expect someone to be standing, sketching."

"A ledge?" O'Connell's interest was piqued. "Could she have fallen from higher up?"

"Could have," Finn conceded, his tone flat. "Or she could have been placed there. The sea, it moves things."

The implication hung in the air, heavy and unspoken. Finn O'Malley was not just a fisherman; he was a man intimately familiar with the sea's power, its capacity to both conceal and reveal. His reluctance to offer more detail, his carefully chosen words, suggested he knew more than he was letting on. He was a witness, but he was also a product of this insular community, bound by unspoken codes of loyalty and silence.

"Did you notice anything unusual about her belongings?" O'Connell asked, recalling the precise arrangement of Gladys's sketchbook, thermos, and bag, juxtaposed with the camera found near her body.

Finn shrugged, his gaze drifting back to his net. "Didn't look. Just saw her. That was enough for me."

O'Connell sensed a wall of polite, yet firm, resistance. Finn, like the others, was protecting something, or someone. The community's collective memory seemed to be a carefully curated collection of stories, with certain chapters deliberately left unwritten.

As O'Connell continued his interviews, a pattern began to emerge. While each villager offered a slightly different perspective on Gladys Quinn, a common thread of guardedness ran through them all. They spoke of her as an artist, a dreamer, an outsider drawn to the raw beauty of their coastline. But beneath the surface of these shared descriptions lay a palpable sense of unease, a quiet suspicion directed not just at O'Connell, but at anything that threatened to disrupt the established order of their lives. The Cailleach's Embrace, a place of both legend and peril, had become the focal point of a mystery that was rapidly deepening, and O'Connell was beginning to suspect that Gladys Quinn's fascination with its secrets had led her to uncover something far more dangerous than a picturesque view. The initial investigations were revealing not a straightforward accident, but a community steeped in its own lore, its own secrets, and its own unspoken loyalties, all of which seemed determined to obscure the truth of Gladys Quinn's final moments. The tide had indeed turned, but not just on the coast; it was turning within the very fabric of Ballyknock, revealing the hidden currents of suspicion and unspoken knowledge that flowed beneath the surface of their seemingly tranquil existence.

Unraveling Gladys' Life

The salt-laced wind that whipped through Ballyknock carried more than just the scent of the sea; it carried whispers of Gladys Quinn's life before she became a tragic footnote in the village's quiet history. Detective O'Connell, a man accustomed to the hard edges of urban crime, found himself navigating a landscape far more nuanced, where the past clung to the present like the persistent mist off the water. His initial conversations in 'The Salty Siren' and with Maeve O'Sullivan had painted a picture of an artist captivated by the wild, untamed spirit of the Cailleach's Embrace. Now, he needed to delve deeper, to excavate the foundations of Gladys's existence, hoping to find the bedrock upon which her final days were built.

He began with the limited personal effects recovered from her rented cottage, a modest dwelling that still held the faint aroma of turpentine and the quiet melancholy of a life cut short. Among her belongings, he found a worn leather-bound journal, its pages filled with a delicate, almost feverish script. These weren't mere diary entries; they were windows into a soul seeking something profound, something beyond the ordinary. The early entries spoke of a deep personal loss, a void left by the sudden death of her younger brother back in Dublin. The details were sparse, but the raw grief was palpable. He had fallen from a cliff during a hike, a senseless accident that had shattered Gladys's world and sent her adrift. The journal chronicled her struggle to navigate the aftermath, the suffocating weight of guilt and the gnawing emptiness that had followed. It was clear that Gladys hadn't just been looking for inspiration in Ballyknock; she had been seeking a form of absolution, a way to reconnect with a life that had suddenly felt fragile and meaningless.

"I can't outrun the silence," one entry read, dated just weeks before her arrival in Ballyknock. "The echo of his last laugh, the image of his face… it's a phantom limb, a constant ache. I keep searching for places that feel solid, places that hold their own stories, hoping they can anchor me. Maybe if I can find a place that's truly alive, truly breathing with its own spirit, I can learn to breathe again myself." This desire for a palpable spiritual connection, a grounding force, explained her intense fascination with the ancient folklore and the raw energy of the coastline.

O'Connell carefully turned the pages, his fingers tracing the lines that spoke of her journey to Ballyknock. "This place," she wrote, "it hums. It's not just the wind or the waves. It's something deeper, something ancient. I feel it in my bones, a resonance that seems to quiet the noise in my head, even if only for a moment. The Cailleach's Embrace… it calls to me. They say it's a place of power, and I believe them. I feel its pull, a magnetic force drawing me in." Her initial impressions were tinged with awe, a sense of discovery that seemed to momentarily lift the cloud of her grief.

Her journal also detailed her research. She had spent hours poring over local archives, the very same ones Liam had mentioned. She was seeking not just artistic inspiration, but historical context, a deeper understanding of the narratives woven into the fabric of the land. "The old maps are fascinating," she'd scribbled. "So many names for the same stretch of coast, shifting with the centuries. 'Cailleach's Embrace' feels the most potent, though. It speaks of a possessiveness, a claim. And the stories of lost souls, of women claimed by the sea… they aren't just tales here, are they? They're memories etched into the very landscape." She seemed to be piecing together a narrative, a tapestry of loss and legend that mirrored her own internal turmoil.

The sketches and photographs that accompanied the journal entries offered a visual counterpoint to her written words. They were a testament to her talent, capturing the rugged beauty of Ballyknock with an artist's eye for light and shadow. But as O'Connell sifted through them, he noticed a subtle shift in their tone and subject matter. The early photographs were expansive landscapes, grand vistas of the sea and sky. Gradually, however, her focus narrowed, becoming more intimate, more focused on the details of the Cailleach's Embrace. Jagged rock formations, the swirling patterns of water in tidal pools, the stark, weathered face of the cliffs – these became her subjects. There was a growing obsession, a deepening fixation on the specific contours of the cove.

He found several sketches that were less about the aesthetic beauty and more about… something else. These were darker, more abstract pieces, filled with swirling lines that suggested movement, perhaps even turmoil. In one, a figure – presumably Gladys herself – was rendered small against the vast, indifferent expanse of the sea, dwarfed by the imposing presence of the cliffs. Around her, the lines seemed to twist and coil, an almost visceral representation of unseen forces. Another sketch depicted a peculiar configuration of rocks, almost like a rough-hewn altar, bathed in an eerie, ethereal light. She had scrawled a single word beside it: "Waiting."

Then came the entries that sent a chill down O'Connell's spine. "I feel watched," she had written, the letters slightly shaky. "Not by people, but by the place itself. It's as if the air is alive, and the stones have eyes. It's unsettling, but also… exhilarating. Like I'm on the cusp of something." This sense of being observed, of a primal awareness emanating from the cove, was a recurring theme in her later writings. It spoke of a growing unease, a primal instinct battling with her artistic curiosity.

Her journal entries became more frequent, more urgent, as the date of her death approached. The tone shifted from one of seeking solace to one of fervent pursuit, almost a desperate need to uncover something. "I think I'm close," she wrote the day before she died. "I feel it in the air, a shift, a revelation waiting to be unveiled. The light this morning was extraordinary, unlike anything I've ever seen. It felt… significant. Like a secret being whispered by the dawn." This premonition of significance, of a profound revelation, mirrored

Liam's account of her excitement about the dawn light at the cove.

But intertwined with this growing anticipation was a deepening sense of dread. "The more I look, the more I feel the weight of it all," she confessed in an entry penned the evening before her death. "The history, the stories, the energy… it's overwhelming. There's a darkness here, too, a counterpoint to the beauty. I know I shouldn't be here, not alone, not digging so deep. But I can't stop. It's like a fever, this need to understand. What is it that the Cailleach guards so fiercely?" The "fever" of her artistic quest, coupled with the growing fear, painted a picture of someone teetering on the edge, both creatively and existentially.

O'Connell also found a small, nondescript digital camera among her belongings. He carefully loaded the memory card, his anticipation mounting. The initial photos were as described: stunning landscapes, intimate studies of the cove's textures, and several shots of Gladys herself, her face etched with concentration as she sketched. But as he scrolled further, he saw images that were taken from a different perspective, as if the camera had been propped up on rocks or placed strategically. These were often shots of the cove from a distance, capturing its vastness and the relentless movement of the sea.

Then, he found a series of photographs that were deeply disturbing. They seemed to have been taken in haste, the composition shaky, the focus often blurred. They depicted fleeting glimpses of shadows moving in the periphery of the frame, figures that were indistinct, almost spectral. In one image, the lens was pointed towards a narrow, almost hidden crevice in the cliff face, the entrance obscured by sea mist. The caption, scrawled in Gladys's distinctive hand on the back of a printed photograph, read: "The mouth of the cave? What's inside?"

Another photograph, taken at dusk, showed the tide pooling around the base of a particularly jagged rock formation. The water seemed unnaturally dark, almost black, and there was a strange, phosphorescent glow emanating from the depths. Gladys had simply written: "Unnatural."

The final images were the most unsettling. They showed Gladys herself, taken from a distance, as if she were being observed. In one, she was sitting on the rocks, sketching, oblivious to the unseen eye. In another, she was walking along the waterline, her back to the camera, moving towards the more secluded part of the cove. The last photograph was a blurry shot of the sea, the focus lost, but a distinct shape, darker than the water, seemed to be just below the surface, moving towards where she had last been seen.

The journal entries and photographs painted a more complex portrait of Gladys Quinn than the simple, melancholic artist the villagers had initially described. She was a woman wrestling with profound grief, seeking spiritual solace, and ultimately, it seemed, stumbling upon something that frightened and fascinated her in equal measure. Her quest for meaning had led her to the Cailleach's Embrace, and in its ancient embrace, she had perhaps found more than just inspiration; she had found secrets that the village, and the sea, had been keeping for a very long time. The feeling of being watched, the glimpses of unseen presences, and the cryptic annotations in her journal all pointed to a growing awareness that her explorations were not merely artistic endeavours but a dangerous delving into the unknown. The tide had indeed turned for Gladys, pulling her into depths that O'Connell now had to navigate. He felt a growing certainty that her death was not an accident, but the culmination of a discovery that had sealed her fate. He needed to understand what Gladys had seen, what she had found, and who or what might have wanted to silence her.

Anomalies at the Scene

The biting wind, a familiar companion in Ballyknock, did little to cool the simmering unease within Detective O'Connell as he stood once more at the Cailleach's Embrace. The tide was out, revealing a treacherous expanse of slick, dark rocks and seaweed-laden pools, the very stage upon which Gladys Quinn's final act had unfolded. He'd walked this shoreline countless times in his mind since reviewing the initial police reports, replaying the gruesome discovery in a loop that offered no comfort, only more questions. Now, with the tangible reality of the scene before him, the abstract uncertainties began to coalesce into something far more concrete, and infinitely more chilling.

He knelt, his gloved fingers tracing the rough, barnacle-encrusted surface of a large boulder that had been noted in the initial forensics report as the general vicinity where Gladys's body had been found. The official narrative was simple, brutal, and tragically plausible: a fall. A slip on the treacherous rocks, an unexpected surge of the tide, a moment of fatal misjudgment in the unforgiving embrace of the coast. Yet, the more O'Connell examined the scant details he possessed, the more that narrative felt like a convenient shroud, pulled taut to conceal something far more sinister.

His gaze drifted to the photograph taken by the responding officer, a stark, grim tableau. Gladys's scarf, a vibrant splash of colour against the muted tones of the rocks and sea, had been tied around her neck. Not a loose, accidental snag, but a knot. A deliberate knot. He leaned closer, his eyes scanning the photographic evidence again, the image now burned into his memory. The knot itself was tight, almost severe. It wasn't the kind of casual tie one might make on a windy day to keep warm or prevent a scarf from being snatched away. It looked… purposeful. And if it was purposeful, then the implication was unavoidable: it had been tied by someone other than Gladys. Or, if by Gladys, then with a motive entirely alien to the circumstances of a casual tumble.

"If she fell," O'Connell murmured to himself, the words snatched away by the wind, "why the knot?" The sheer irrationality of it gnawed at him. A person falling, struggling against the elements, would likely be dislodging anything tied around their neck, not securing it further. Unless, of course, the fall wasn't the primary event. Unless the knot was an attempt to silence, to bind, before the final act. He pictured Gladys, perhaps struggling against an unseen assailant, the scarf a tool of coercion. The thought sent a shiver, cold and sharp, down his spine.

He moved his attention to the camera, a small, dark object recovered near her. The angle at which it had been found, nestled amongst the jagged stones, had seemed innocuous enough in the initial reports. Just another piece of equipment lost in the chaos of a fatal accident. But O'Connell was no longer interested in innocuous. He remembered the blurry final photograph, the one where the lens seemed to have lost focus, pointed towards the churning water. Had the camera been dropped? Or had it been placed? And if placed, by whom? And to what end? He visualized Gladys's last moments, her frantic struggle, or perhaps, her desperate attempt to document something before it was too late. The angle of the camera, he now realized, was odd. It wasn't lying haphazardly, as if dropped from a height. It was propped, almost carefully, against a cluster of smaller rocks, tilted upwards towards the sea. It suggested a deliberate act, an attempt to capture a specific view, or perhaps, to record something for posterity, even in the face of imminent danger.

Then there was the mark. It had been dismissed as a minor abrasion, consistent with scraping against the rocks during a fall. But O'Connell's instincts, honed by years of observing the subtle tells of violence, screamed otherwise. He'd seen the forensic sketches, the close-ups of Gladys's left wrist. It was a faint, reddish mark, a series of small, parallel lines. Not a tear from fabric, not a jagged gash from a sharp rock. It looked... deliberate. Like the imprint of something small, something that had been pressed firmly against her skin. He zoomed in on the digital copy of the photograph, his brow furrowed in concentration. The lines were too regular, too evenly spaced to be accidental. They were more akin to a brand, or perhaps, the impression left by a tight grip, the edges of fingers digging in. But there was no bruising, no swelling around the mark, which seemed inconsistent with a violent struggle. What kind of pressure would leave such a distinct mark without causing more extensive damage? It was a subtle detail, easily overlooked, but it was a thread, however thin, that O'Connell felt compelled to pull.

The landscape itself, he now realized, was a complicit party to the deception. The Cailleach's Embrace was a place of natural hazards, a symphony of shifting sands, treacherous currents, and razor-sharp rocks that were constantly being reshaped by the relentless power of the Atlantic. It was a place that could indeed conceal the truth, a labyrinth of shadows and deceptive appearances. The tide, that capricious force, could erase evidence with the swiftness of a magician's trick, washing away footprints, scattering debris, leaving behind only the stark, indifferent remnants of nature's fury. But O'Connell was beginning to suspect that this 'natural' destruction had been aided by human intervention.

He walked along the waterline, the retreating waves licking at his boots. He scanned the rock face, looking for anything out of the ordinary, any small detail that the initial investigators might have missed in their rush to confirm the accidental death. Gladys's journal entries had spoken of caves, of hidden crevices. Had she found one? Had she ventured into a place where she shouldn't have? The photograph of the narrow crevice, captioned "The mouth of the cave? What's inside?", flashed in his mind. He looked towards the section of the cliff face where such a crevice might exist, the shadows deepening as the sun began its slow descent towards the horizon. The unforgiving terrain offered countless such nooks and crannies, each a potential hiding place, a potential tomb.

The concept of 'unnatural' had been Gladys's word, scribbled beside the photograph of the dark, phosphorescent water. O'Connell tried to recall the exact location shown in the image. It was a tidal pool, he believed, trapped amongst the rocks as the tide receded. He squinted, trying to orient himself, to match the photographic perspective with the reality before him. He found a likely candidate, a deep, dark pool, its surface unnervingly still, reflecting the bruised sky above. He couldn't see any phosphorescence now, but that was hardly surprising. The sea was a capricious mistress, its moods and phenomena often fleeting. Yet, the word stuck with him. Unnatural. What had she seen that had prompted such a stark, and unsettling, observation?

He knelt by the edge of the pool, peering into its murky depths. The water was frigid, the smell of brine and decaying seaweed heavy in the air. He saw no unusual glow, no sign of anything out of the ordinary. But the very stillness of the water, in such a tempestuous environment, felt like a subtle anomaly. It was as if the sea itself was holding its breath, concealing a secret beneath its dark surface. He ran his hand along the edge of the pool, the rocks slick with a fine, almost greasy film. It wasn't the usual slime of algae; it felt different, more viscous. He brought his fingers to his nose, sniffing cautiously. A faint, metallic scent, almost imperceptible, clung to his fingertips. It wasn't the rust of iron; it was something sharper, more acrid.

The presence of this unusual residue, coupled with Gladys's cryptic annotation, planted a seed of doubt that began to blossom into a full-blown conviction. This wasn't just a tragedy; it was a carefully orchestrated deception. The inconsistencies he had noted – the scarf's knot, the camera's placement, the mark on Gladys's wrist, and now this strange film in the tidal pool – all pointed towards a narrative far removed from the one presented to him. Gladys Quinn had not simply succumbed to the unforgiving elements. She had, it seemed, stumbled upon something that someone was desperate to keep hidden, and her death was not an accident, but an act of calculated silencing. The tide had turned, not just for Gladys, but for O'Connell's investigation, pushing him towards the treacherous depths of a man-made mystery. He had to understand what Gladys had seen, what she had touched, what she had discovered in the shadowed embrace of the Cailleach's domain. And he had to find out who had gone to such lengths to ensure her silence, ensuring that the secrets of Ballyknock remained buried beneath the unforgiving waves.

He continued his methodical circuit of the area, his eyes scanning the ground, the rocks, the cliff face. He looked for anything that seemed out of place, anything that the initial sweep might have missed. He circled back to the spot where Gladys's body had been found, picturing her lying there, the sea receding around her. He imagined the scene as it might have been before the first responders arrived, before the tide began its relentless work of erasure. What would have been visible then, that was no longer visible now?

His gaze fell upon a cluster of rocks, slightly further from the main area of discovery, closer to the base of the cliff. They were unremarkable at first glance, just more of the same weathered granite. But as he looked closer, he noticed a faint scuff mark on one of the flatter surfaces, a mark that seemed too precise, too linear to be the result of natural erosion or the chaotic tumbling of debris during a storm. It was a faint scratch, almost like something had been dragged across the rock. He knelt again, running his finger along the mark. It was shallow, but distinct. And it led, he noticed, towards a narrow fissure in the cliff face, partially obscured by a curtain of sea-worn ivy.

This was it. This was the crevice Gladys had photographed, the one she'd questioned. He remembered the caption: "The mouth of the cave? What's inside?" He pulled a powerful flashlight from his kit, its beam cutting a sharp swathe through the encroaching twilight. He carefully pushed aside the ivy, revealing a dark, forbidding opening, no wider than a man's shoulders. A faint, cool draft emanated from within, carrying with it a peculiar scent – damp earth, yes, but also something else, something faintly chemical, almost like ozone, and a hint of the metallic tang he had noticed at the tidal pool.

He hesitated for only a moment. The thought of entering an unknown, potentially unstable cave, especially as the tide was beginning to turn again, was not a decision to be taken lightly. But O'Connell knew, with a certainty that settled deep in his gut, that this was where the answers lay. Gladys's journal, her photographs, her final, desperate words – they all pointed to this hidden place. This was not merely an anomaly; it was the heart of the mystery.

Taking a deep breath, he switched on his flashlight and ducked into the opening. The passage was narrow, forcing him to move sideways, his shoulders brushing against the cold, damp rock. The air grew heavier, the scent more pronounced. The beam of his flashlight danced ahead, illuminating a rough-hewn tunnel that seemed to descend deeper into the cliff. Water dripped from the ceiling, echoing in the confined space. After a few yards, the passage widened slightly, opening into a small, natural chamber. The floor was uneven, littered with pebbles and fragments of shell.

His flashlight beam swept across the chamber, and he froze. There, against the far wall, lay something that made his blood run cold. It was a small, canvas bag, of the type an artist might use to carry supplies. It was partially open, and its contents were spilling out onto the damp rock floor. Among them, he could make out tubes of paint, charcoal sticks, and a few crumpled sheets of paper. But it was what lay beneath the canvas bag that truly seized his attention.

It was a small, intricately carved wooden box, dark with age and moisture. It looked old, very old. And beside it, half-buried in the gravel, was a single, tarnished silver locket. His heart pounded in his chest. He reached out, his fingers trembling slightly as he picked up the locket. It was cool to the touch. He managed to pry it open. Inside, faded but still discernible, were two miniature portraits: a young woman with dark, coiled hair, and a man with a stern, unsmiling face. He didn't recognize them. They were too old, too stylized to be from recent memory.

He then turned his attention to the wooden box. It was locked, a small, rusted clasp holding it shut. He needed to get it open. He rummaged through the canvas bag and found a small palette knife, its edge sharp. With careful pressure, he worked at the clasp. It groaned, then gave way with a faint click. He lifted the lid.

Inside, nestled on a bed of faded velvet, was not treasure, not jewels, but something far more significant to his investigation. There were several small, rolled-up scrolls, tied with faded ribbon, and a collection of what appeared to be dried herbs, their scent faint but distinct. He carefully unrolled one of the scrolls. The writing was archaic, written in a spidery, faded ink, and the language was... Latin. He recognised a few words, but the context was lost on him. He unrolled another. This one contained a crude map, or perhaps a diagram, of the coastline, with several points marked with strange symbols.

Then, his flashlight beam landed on something else within the box, something that made the metallic scent in the air seem to intensify. It was a small, wickedly sharp knife, its blade stained a dark, rusty colour. He picked it up, examining it carefully. It was unlike any ordinary knife he had ever seen. The blade was narrow and curved, almost like a surgical instrument, or perhaps, a ritualistic blade. And on the handle, intricately carved, was a symbol he recognized from Gladys's sketches – a coiled serpent.

The realization hit him with the force of a physical blow. Gladys hadn't just been an artist drawn to the folklore of Ballyknock. She had been actively seeking something, something hidden within these ancient caves, something connected to the village's shadowed past. The scrolls, the herbs, the archaic map, the strange knife – these were not the accoutrements of a casual hiker or a plein-air painter. They spoke of a deliberate, perhaps even desperate, search for knowledge, for understanding, or perhaps, for something more arcane.

The mark on her wrist... what if it wasn't from a struggle, but from handling these items? What if she had been trying to open the box, or had been pricked by the knife? The "unnatural" glow in the tidal pool, the metallic scent – could it be related to the contents of this box, or what had been done with them? The pieces were beginning to fit together, forming a picture that was far more complex and dangerous than he could have imagined. Gladys Quinn's death was not an accident. It was the culmination of a discovery, a discovery that had unearthed secrets the people of Ballyknock, or at least some of them, were willing to kill to protect. The Anomalies at the Scene were not random; they were carefully placed breadcrumbs, leading to a truth that was as dark and as deep as the sea itself. He had to understand what Gladys had found in this hidden chamber, and what it meant for her, and for Ballyknock. The tide had truly turned, revealing a monstrous undertow.

CHAPTER THREE — THE SHADOWS OF THE PAST

Maeves Ancient Lore

The salt-laden wind whipped O'Connell's coat around him as he made his way through Ballyknock's narrow, winding lanes. The late afternoon sun cast long, distorted shadows, and an early autumn chill had settled over the village. His steps carried him towards a small, stone cottage nestled on the outskirts, its chimney emitting a thin plume of smoke that promised warmth and, more importantly, answers. Maeve O'Malley was Ballyknock's keeper of secrets, its living repository of ancient lore and forgotten tales. If anyone could shed light on the unsettling currents O'Connell felt swirling around Gladys Quinn's death, it would be the woman who seemed to breathe the very history of the place.

He found her tending to a small garden, her hands, gnarled by age and work, meticulously pulling weeds from around a patch of hardy herbs. Her face, etched with the lines of a life lived close to the land and its stories, turned towards him as he approached. There was a knowing glint in her faded blue eyes, a recognition that went beyond his official capacity as a detective. She seemed to understand the weight he carried before he even spoke.

"Detective O'Connell," she greeted him, her voice raspy, like dry leaves skittering across stone. "I've been expecting you."

O'Connell paused, the unexpectedness of her statement momentarily disarming him. "Expecting me? How so, Maeve?"

She wiped her hands on her apron and gestured for him to follow her inside. The cottage was small but densely packed with the artifacts of a lifetime devoted to the past. Bookshelves overflowed with ancient-looking tomes, their spines cracked and their pages brittle. Maps, some hand-drawn, others faded reproductions, adorned the walls, depicting coastlines and ancient settlements long since vanished. The air was thick with the scent of dried herbs, old paper, and a faint, earthy aroma that O'Connell couldn't quite place.

"This village," Maeve began, settling into a worn armchair by the hearth, her gaze distant, as if peering into a different era, "it whispers its secrets to those who know how to listen. And it has been whispering about Gladys Quinn. About her... fascination."

O'Connell sat opposite her, his notebook open on his lap, his pen poised. "Her fascination? She was an artist, Maeve. She was drawn to the beauty of the coastline, the local legends."

Maeve let out a dry chuckle that held no amusement. "Beauty, yes. But Gladys was not content with merely observing. She dug. She delved. She sought the bones beneath the skin of these stories. And some bones are best left undisturbed, Detective."

She rose and moved towards a large, leather-bound volume resting on a sturdy wooden table. Its cover was unadorned, its pages thick and yellowed. She opened it with a reverence that O'Connell found both intriguing and unsettling.

"The Cailleach's Embrace," Maeve began, her voice dropping to a near whisper, "is more than just a dramatic stretch of coastline. It is a place of power, a nexus where the ancient world still breathes. Centuries ago, long before Ballyknock was even a whisper on the wind, this cove was a sacred site. It was where the Veil between our world and the world of the 'Other' was thinnest."

She ran a finger over an elaborate, ink-drawn illustration within the book – a depiction of a rugged coastline, with a distinct indentation that mirrored the familiar shape of Cailleach's Embrace.

"The old ways were strong then," she continued. "The people understood the forces that shaped their lives, the capricious nature of the sea, the unpredictable bounty of the land. And they understood the need for balance. When the sea grew wrathful, when the storms raged with unnatural fury, when the fish refused to swim and the crops withered, they knew they had to appease the powers that be."

O'Connell leaned forward, his senses heightened. This was precisely the kind of deep-rooted lore he had hoped Maeve would provide. The official report had been clinical, factual, devoid of any such historical context.

"And how did they appease these powers, Maeve?" he prompted gently.

Maeve's gaze fixed on the illustration, her brow furrowed with a mixture of awe and apprehension. "There are tales… old tales, passed down through whispers and fragmented songs, of a sacrifice. A priestess, chosen for her purity and her connection to the land, would be offered to the sea. A tribute, to calm the wrath, to ensure the continuation of life."

The word 'sacrifice' hung in the air, heavy and chilling. O'Connell's mind immediately flashed to the knot on Gladys's scarf, the mark on her wrist, the unsettling stillness of the tidal pool.

"A priestess?" O'Connell echoed, trying to keep his voice steady. "What was her name?"

"The stories vary," Maeve said, her voice almost a sigh. "Some call her the 'Sea Maiden,' others the 'Caller of Tides.' But the most persistent legend speaks of a priestess named Sorcha. Her name, in the old tongue, meant 'brightness,' or 'light.' A poignant irony, given her fate."

Maeve's gaze met O'Connell's, and in her eyes, he saw not just the recounting of a myth, but a deep, visceral fear. "Sorcha was said to be beautiful, with hair like spun moonlight and eyes the colour of the deepest ocean. She was beloved by her people, but she was also chosen. Chosen to walk the path of the sacred offering."

She turned another page in the ancient tome, revealing more intricate drawings and faded script. "The ritual was complex, steeped in ancient rites. It was not a brutal act of violence, but a solemn communion. Sorcha would be led to the very edge of the Embrace, adorned with garlands of seaweed and shells. She would sing a lament, a song of farewell and of hope, to the churning waters. And then... then she would walk into the sea, a willing offering to ensure the prosperity of her people."

O'Connell absorbed her words, his mind trying to reconcile this ancient tale with the brutal reality of Gladys's death. Was there a connection? Could a centuries-old ritual still hold sway in the modern world?

"But Maeve," he interjected, his voice laced with a healthy dose of skepticism, "this is a legend. A myth. How can it possibly relate to Gladys's death?"

Maeve's expression hardened slightly, her gaze sharpening. "Legends are not born from nothing, Detective. They are echoes of truth, amplified by time and fear. The people of Ballyknock, for generations, believed that by honoring this ancient ritual, by respecting the sanctity of the Cailleach's Embrace, they maintained a delicate balance. They appeased a powerful, ancient entity that resided in the depths, a deity that predated even the oldest Celtic gods."

She pointed to a section of text that was more densely written, the ink darker and more elaborate. "This passage speaks of a protective ward, a curse laid upon the land by Sorcha herself, or by those who mourned her. It was meant to safeguard the sacred site, to deter anyone who sought to disturb the ancient balance, to disrupt the slumber of the entity in the deep. Anyone who tread too carelessly, who sought to uncover what was buried, would incur its displeasure."

A shiver traced its way down O'Connell's spine. Gladys's relentless pursuit of the cove's history, her deep dives into its folklore, her cryptic journal entries – they all spoke of someone who was, perhaps, treading too carelessly.

"You believe Gladys disturbed this balance, Maeve?" he asked, his voice hushed.

Maeve nodded slowly, her eyes fixed on the open book. "Gladys was… unusually drawn to the Embrace. More so than any artist before her. She spoke of a feeling, a presence. She felt that the land itself was calling to her, revealing its secrets. She spent hours there, sketching, observing, searching for the source of the 'unnatural' phenomena she documented. She was looking for the heart of the old stories."

She paused, her gaze drifting towards the window, as if seeing beyond the mundane reality of the village. "And I believe, Detective, that in her fervent search, she may have inadvertently awakened something. Something ancient and primal, something that had long been dormant. The protective curse, meant to ward off those who merely passed through, would have been amplified for someone who actively sought to disturb the very foundations of its power."

O'Connell's mind raced. The mark on Gladys's wrist – could it have been a sigil, a mark of possession or claim? The strange metallic scent at the tidal pool and in the cave – was it some residual energy, some manifestation of this ancient entity? And the knot on her scarf… a desperate attempt to ward off something, or a symbol of an ancient ritual?

"Maeve," he said, his voice firm, "what do you know about this 'entity'? What was it that the priestess was meant to appease?"

Maeve hesitated, her gaze flicking back to the book, her expression one of deep unease. "The old tales are fragmented, Detective. They speak of a 'Mother of the Tides,' a being of immense power, tied to the very essence of the ocean. Some describe her as benevolent, providing bounty and protection. Others, particularly when angered, depict her as a force of absolute destruction, capable of swallowing entire villages. It is said she slumbered in the deepest trench off the coast, her dreams shaping the currents, her moods dictating the fate of those who lived by the sea."

She tapped a finger on a faded passage. "This scroll here," she indicated a small, rolled parchment tucked within the pages, "speaks of a time when the entity was angered by the transgressions of mankind. It was then that the priestess Sorcha was chosen. The sacrifice was not merely an appeasement, but a binding. A way to ensure that the entity remained bound to its domain, its power contained, its influence over the human world limited."

O'Connell felt a growing sense of dread. Gladys hadn't just been researching local legends; she had stumbled upon a narrative that was potentially still alive, still potent.

"And the curse?" he pressed. "What did it entail?"

"It was a binding of intention, Detective," Maeve explained, her voice low and resonant. "A spiritual chain woven into the very fabric of the land around the Embrace. It was meant to instill a sense of dread, a subconscious revulsion, in those who harbored ill intent or sought to exploit the ancient power. But for someone like Gladys, who approached with reverence, with a genuine desire to understand, it may have acted differently. Perhaps it served as a beacon, drawing her deeper into the secrets, inadvertently triggering the dormant forces."

She looked directly at O'Connell, her eyes holding a profound sadness. "Gladys was drawn to the power, Detective. She felt it, she understood it on an intuitive level. But understanding is one thing. Awakening it is another. And the price for awakening something so ancient, so untamed, can be terrible."

Maeve then described the significance of certain local landmarks that Gladys had obsessively sketched in her journal – peculiar rock formations, ancient standing stones rumoured to exist near the coast, the very crevice O'Connell had discovered. "These places," she explained, "were part of the ancient rituals, markers of the sacred boundaries. The standing stones, for instance, were believed to be focal points for channeling energy. The crevice… some legends say it was a passage, a gateway to the 'Other' realm, guarded by Sorcha's spirit."

She spoke of the "Sea Witch," another local moniker for a figure associated with the cove, a sorceress who was said to control the tides and summon storms. While distinct from the priestess, the folklore seemed to weave together, a tapestry of fear and reverence for the potent forces of the sea. Maeve suggested that Gladys's deep dive into these seemingly disparate legends might have been her way of piecing together a larger, more terrifying truth – a truth that had been deliberately obscured by the village's collective memory, a truth that some might still wish to keep buried.

"The folklore," Maeve concluded, her voice barely audible above the crackling fire, "is a warning. It tells of a power that demands respect, a balance that must be maintained. Gladys, with her artist's soul and her historian's mind, touched that power. And I fear, Detective, that she paid the ultimate price for disturbing its slumber."

O'Connell sat in silence for a long moment, the weight of Maeve's words settling upon him. The ancient lore, once dismissed as mere superstition, now seemed to cast a chillingly plausible shadow over Gladys Quinn's demise. The priestess, the sacrifice, the curse – these were not just stories anymore. They were potential explanations, a framework for understanding the anomalies that had gnawed at his instincts from the very beginning. He had come seeking historical context, and he had found a narrative that was far more profound, and far more terrifying, than he could have ever anticipated. He knew, with a growing certainty, that the answers to Gladys Quinn's death lay not just in the present, but in the echoes of a forgotten past, a past that still held a potent, and dangerous, grip on Ballyknock.

Finns Cryptic Warnings

O'Connell left Maeve's cottage with a mind reeling. The ancient tales of priestesses and appeasement were a far cry from the forensic reports he was accustomed to, yet they resonated with a primal truth that unsettled him deeply. He needed another perspective, someone who lived by the sea and understood its moods not through dusty tomes, but through a lifetime of direct, unvarnished experience. Finn was that man. The fisherman, a man as weathered and taciturn as the rocks of the coast itself, was Ballyknock's silent observer, his life dictated by the rhythm of the tides and the unpredictable bounty of the ocean.

He found Finn down at the harbour, mending nets with a practiced, almost meditative rhythm. The salt spray kissed O'Connell's face as he approached, the sharp tang of brine a stark contrast to the earthy scents of Maeve's cottage. Finn's hands, calloused and strong, moved with an economy of motion that spoke of years spent wrestling a living from the unforgiving sea. His eyes, the colour of a stormy sea, flickered up as O'Connell drew near, a flicker of recognition, then a return to his task.

"Finn," O'Connell began, his voice carrying over the gentle creak of the boats and the distant cry of gulls. "A moment of your time, if you have it."

Finn grunted, not looking up. His focus remained on the intricate knot he was tying, a precise weave of twine that would hold fast against the pull of the ocean. "Time is for catchin'," Finn replied, his voice a low rumble, like pebbles shifting on the seabed. "Or for mendin' what the catch takes from ye."

O'Connell leaned against a nearby bollard, the cold metal seeping through his coat. He understood Finn's reticence. The sea held its own secrets, and men like Finn were often reluctant to share them, especially with outsiders. "I'm asking about Gladys Quinn."

At the mention of her name, Finn's hands stilled for a fraction of a second. His gaze, however, remained fixed on the net. "Artist," Finn stated, as if that explained everything.

"She was," O'Connell agreed. "But she spent a lot of time near the coves, didn't she? Near the Embrace."

Finn's shoulders tensed almost imperceptibly. He finally looked up, his eyes meeting O'Connell's with an intensity that belied his usual monosyllabic responses. There was a wariness in that gaze, a caution born of experience. "The sea," Finn said, his voice a low growl, "she takes what she wants. And she gives what she pleases. Ye don't question the ways of the sea."

"But you saw things, didn't you, Finn?" O'Connell pressed, his own gaze steady. "In the days before she disappeared. Unusual things?"

Finn let out a long, slow breath, the sound mingling with the sigh of the waves against the quay. He glanced towards the horizon, where the sky was beginning to bleed into hues of orange and purple, and the sea itself seemed to churn with a restless energy. "Tides," he said finally, his voice barely above a whisper, as if the words themselves were too heavy to speak aloud. "They were... unnatural. Pulling hard, then slackening with no reason. Like a breath held too long, then exhaled with a sigh."

O'Connell scribbled in his notebook. Unnatural tides. Maeve had spoken of the sea's power, of the entity that slumbered in the depths. Could these anomalies be connected? "And lights?" O'Connell prompted. "Did you see any strange lights near the cove?"

Finn's eyes narrowed, scanning the darkening water. "Aye. Flickers. Like phosphorescence, but... sharper. Too steady. Out near the rocks where the water's deepest. Dancing in the twilight, they were. Not the usual shimmer from the shoals. Something... else." He paused, his jaw tightening. "Something that made the hairs on the back of your neck stand up."

O'Connell felt a prickle of unease. Strange lights. Unnatural tides. He pictured Gladys, alone, sketching near the very spot Finn was describing. "Did you see Gladys near there, Finn? In the days before she vanished?"

Finn hesitated. His gaze drifted back to the sea, a silent communion with its depths. He seemed to be wrestling with something, with a reluctant memory. "Night before she went missing," Finn said, his voice strained. "Saw her. On the cliff path. Near the old standing stones."

O'Connell's pen hovered above his notebook. This was new. "You saw her? With someone?"

Finn's knuckles were white as he gripped the net. He took another deep, ragged breath. "There was… a figure. With her. Tall. Hard to make out in the gloom. Cloaked, maybe. Met her there. Spoke for a bit. Then they walked down towards the water's edge." His voice dropped, laced with a regret O'Connell couldn't quite decipher. "Couldn't see the face. Too dark. But they went down. Towards the Embrace."

O'Connell felt a surge of adrenaline. A stranger. The last person to see Gladys alive, and a stranger at that. "Could you describe this person at all, Finn? Anything? Male? Female? What were they wearing?"

Finn shook his head, his gaze distant, fixed on a memory that clearly troubled him. "Just… a shadow. A shape against the fading light. But they seemed… drawn to the place. Or maybe they *belonged* there. Like they knew the path, the secrets of that stretch." He looked back at O'Connell, his eyes holding a depth of unspoken knowledge. "Some folks, Detective, they have an understanding with the sea. An old pact. They hear its whispers when others hear only the wind."

O'Connell's mind raced. Maeve's ancient priestess, Sorcha, her pact with the sea. Finn's words, though sparse, painted a picture of Gladys meeting someone who was as much a part of the cove as the rocks and the waves. It wasn't just a chance encounter; it felt deliberate, almost ritualistic. The stranger, the cliff path, the descent towards the water's edge. It painted a grim tableau, one that was undeniably linked to the folklore Maeve had so vividly described.

"You didn't report seeing this person, Finn?" O'Connell asked, his tone gentle, not accusatory. He understood the unwritten codes of Ballyknock, the deep-seated distrust of authority that often kept its secrets buried.

Finn finally met his gaze, his expression etched with a weariness that went beyond physical exertion. "What good would it have done?" he asked, his voice rough. "Sayin' I saw a shape on the cliff? Against the sea? The sea... she don't answer to constables, Detective. She has her own keepers." He gestured vaguely towards the dark expanse of the ocean. "Some things... some things are meant to stay hidden. Like treasures at the bottom of a deep trench. Trying to pull them up... it stirs up more than you bargain for."

The implication hung heavy in the salty air. Finn was not just a fisherman; he was a guardian of sorts, a silent observer who understood that some forces were best left undisturbed. His cryptic warnings, delivered with the stoicism of a man who had faced the sea's fury countless times, resonated with the unsettling narrative Maeve had woven. Gladys hadn't just been an artist drawn to pretty landscapes; she had been delving into something ancient, something powerful, and perhaps, in the twilight of that fateful evening, she had met someone who was intimately connected to that very power. The stranger on the cliff, the unnatural tides, the strange lights – they were pieces of a puzzle that O'Connell was only just beginning to assemble, a puzzle where the edges were blurred by the encroaching darkness and the secrets whispered by the restless sea. The question gnawed at him: was the stranger a threat, a protector, or something else entirely, a harbinger of the ancient forces Finn and Maeve both alluded to?

The Villages Collective Secret

The air in Ballyknock, thick with the scent of salt and damp earth, seemed to carry more than just the usual maritime aromas. Detective O'Connell felt it – a palpable reticence, a collective holding of breath that settled over the village like a shroud. Every conversation, every sideways glance, every carefully chosen word was a testament to a shared understanding, an unspoken agreement to keep certain truths buried deeper than any shipwreck. It was a conspiracy of silence, not born of malice, but of a deep-seated, perhaps inherited, instinct for self-preservation, a learned response to a life lived in the shadow of the sea's formidable power.

He'd started, as any investigator would, by canvassing the village, knocking on doors, asking questions that, in his experience, usually elicited at least a modicum of candidness, even if reluctant. Here, however, his inquiries about Gladys Quinn, about her solitary walks and her fascination with the local coves, were met with a polite, almost practiced, blankness. The villagers spoke of Gladys as a lovely, talented young woman, a gifted artist who captured the rugged beauty of Ballyknock on her canvases. But beyond that, there was a wall. A courteous, impenetrable wall.

Mrs. Gable, a woman whose age seemed to be etched into the very fabric of her rosy cheeks, her hands perpetually busy with knitting even as she spoke, offered a typical response. "Gladys? Oh, a dear girl. Such a shame, such a terrible shame. The sea… it's a cruel mistress, Detective. Takes what she wants, and no amount of asking will bring it back." Her needles clicked with a steady, rhythmic cadence, a sound that seemed to punctuate her words, each click a small, deliberate dismissal of further inquiry.

"She spent a lot of time down by the cliffs, Mrs. Gable," O'Connell prompted, leaning forward slightly. "Near what they call the 'Embrace'."

Mrs. Gable's eyes, the colour of faded denim, flickered momentarily, a spark of something – unease? recognition? – before settling back into a placid, uninformative gaze. "The cliffs are beautiful, Detective. Artists are drawn to beauty, aren't they? It's only natural." She offered a tight, thin smile. "She was a soul who loved the wild places."

It was the same everywhere. Young Liam, who worked the fishing boats with Finn, his face still unlined by the harsh realities of the sea, stammered his way through a denial of seeing anything unusual. "Gladys? Nah, sir. Just... painting. Always painting." His eyes, however, darted nervously towards the harbour, as if seeking a silent confirmation from the bobbing vessels. O'Connell noted the tremor in his voice, the way his gaze refused to meet his own directly.

Even old Mr. Crowley, the retired lighthouse keeper, a man who had seen decades of storms and shifting tides from his solitary perch, offered only platitudes. "The sea has its ways, Detective. Always has. Some souls are just... called to it, I suppose. Like the tides themselves." He'd spoken with a wistful faraway look, as if recalling a personal, private connection to the ocean's mystery.

It wasn't just that they were withholding information; it was the way they did it. There was no overt hostility, no anger. Instead, it was a seamless tapestry of deflection and vague pronouncements, a shared language of allusion and implication that O'Connell, an outsider, struggled to decipher. He sensed a deep current of shared history running beneath the surface of their polite refusals, a history that bound them together in a silent pact. They were a community, and like any tight-knit community, they protected their own, and perhaps, their own secrets.

His earlier conversation with Finn, the taciturn fisherman, had provided a glimpse into this deeper undercurrent. Finn's mention of "unnatural tides" and "strange lights" had been a crack in the facade, a hint of the anomalies that might have accompanied Gladys's disappearance. But even Finn, O'Connell suspected, had revealed only what he deemed absolutely necessary, his words carefully weighed, his silences pregnant with unsaid things. Finn had alluded to a deeper knowledge, an "understanding with the sea," and O'Connell realised that this understanding extended to the community as a whole.

He began to notice a pattern, a subtle but persistent echo in the villagers' retellings. A few years prior, a young man, a visitor to the village, had drowned near the same cove. The official verdict had been a tragic accident, a rogue wave, the sea claiming another life. But O'Connell found whispers, dismissed as local folklore or the ramblings of grief-stricken relatives, that hinted at something more. They spoke of the young man's obsession with the very same standing stones Gladys had been drawn to, his fascination with the local legends that Maeve, the village elder, had alluded to.

Then there was the incident two decades ago, a fisherman lost at sea. His boat had been found adrift, sails shredded, but with no sign of the man. The official report cited a sudden squall, a violent storm. Yet, O'Connell unearthed old newspaper clippings, fragments of hushed conversations from a time before he'd even arrived in Ballyknock, that spoke of strange lights in the sky that night, of the sea behaving in an erratic, unsettling manner, eerily similar to Finn's description of the tides around the time of Gladys's disappearance.

These weren't isolated incidents. They were threads in a larger narrative, a tapestry of loss woven into the fabric of Ballyknock's existence. Each event, while officially chalked up to the sea's capricious nature, carried with it a faint, persistent murmur of something extraordinary, something inexplicable. The villagers, in their shared reticence, seemed to be collectively preserving a narrative, a story that acknowledged the sea's power but perhaps shielded a more specific, more human, explanation for these tragedies.

O'Connell visited the local Garda station, a small, unassuming building that seemed more like a glorified post office. He pored over old case files, the brittle paper whispering tales of lives claimed by the unforgiving Atlantic. The reports were maddeningly consistent in their brevity and their reliance on natural explanations. Drowning. Lost at sea. Accident. The language was sterile, clinical, a stark contrast to the raw, emotional weight of each disappearance. It was as if the authorities, too, had accepted Ballyknock's narrative of the sea's inherent danger, a convenient explanation that required no deeper probing.

He found a notation in one of the older files, a brief mention by a visiting inspector from years past, expressing a "curious lack of substantive witness accounts" in a particular case, noting the "unusual reticence of the local populace." The inspector had made a recommendation for further inquiry, but the file ended there, the recommendation seemingly lost in the bureaucratic shuffle. It was a small crack, a fleeting acknowledgement from an outsider that something was amiss, something the villagers actively, if passively, concealed.

O'Connell realised that his investigation into Gladys Quinn's disappearance was becoming an excavation into the village's collective memory, or perhaps, its collective amnesia.

The silence wasn't just a refusal to speak; it was an active participation in a shared narrative. They were custodians of a secret, passed down through generations, a story woven with fear, superstition, and perhaps, a deep-seated understanding of the forces at play in their isolated corner of the world.

He revisited Maeve. Her small cottage, smelling of peat smoke and dried herbs, felt like a sanctuary from the veiled hostility he'd encountered elsewhere. Maeve, her face a roadmap of a life lived close to the earth and the sea, listened patiently as he recounted his conversations, the pattern of evasion he'd encountered.

"They are afraid, Detective," Maeve said, her voice soft but firm, her gaze unwavering. "Not of you, perhaps, but of what you might unearth. Ballyknock has always kept its own counsel. The sea... it is not just water and waves to us. It is life, yes, but it is also... older than us. And it demands respect. A certain... deference."

"Deference?" O'Connell probed. "Or complicity?"

Maeve stirred the embers in the hearth, a shower of sparks momentarily illuminating her weathered features. "The lines blur, Detective, when the boundary between the known and the unknowable becomes so thin. They have seen things, these people. They have heard things whispered on the wind, seen shapes in the mist that the rational mind rejects. To speak of those things openly is to invite them closer, to give them power."

She spoke of the 'sea-kin,' of ancient pacts and offerings made to appease the ocean's slumbering power. These weren't mere folklore for the villagers; they were ingrained beliefs, a practical theology that guided their lives. "The sea takes its toll," she repeated Finn's words, but with a different emphasis. "It is a price paid for living on its doorstep. And sometimes," her voice dropped, a hint of sorrow colouring her tone, "sometimes the price is steeper than others. When someone crosses a boundary, a line that should not be crossed, the sea… it corrects. It reclaims what is not truly its own, but what it has been permitted to hold."

O'Connell felt a chill that had nothing to do with the sea air. "What boundary are we talking about, Maeve? And who decides when it's crossed?"

Maeve finally looked directly at him, her eyes holding a profound sadness. "Gladys was an artist, yes. But she was also… a seeker. She looked too deeply into the old places, into the heart of the Embrace. She asked questions that the sea does not like to be asked. She was drawn to its mysteries, and perhaps, it was drawn to her. But not in the way you might think. Not as a lover, Detective. More like a predator."

The collected silence of the village, O'Connell now understood, was a shield. It was their way of acknowledging the unspoken rule: the sea's secrets, and by extension, the village's secrets, were not to be trifled with. The repeated 'accidents' were not mere statistical anomalies; they were part of a larger, unwritten history that the villagers guarded fiercely. Their silence was a testament to their shared burden, a collective agreement to let the waves wash over the truth, to allow the ocean's vast indifference to serve as their alibi.

He knew then that his path forward wouldn't be paved with official statements and forensic evidence alone. He would have to navigate the treacherous currents of Ballyknock's collective consciousness, to understand the unspoken language of their shared fear and their inherited knowledge. Gladys Quinn hadn't just vanished; she had stepped into a story that had been unfolding for centuries, a story whispered by the tides and guarded by the silent, watchful eyes of the village. And O'Connell, the outsider, was now inextricably caught in its undertow, a lone figure against the unified, enduring silence of Ballyknock. He would need to find a way to break through that wall, not by force, but by understanding, by uncovering the kernel of truth that lay buried beneath their shared, ancestral secret. The investigation had deepened, transforming from a search for a missing person into an exploration of a community's soul, a soul inextricably bound to the ancient, powerful mysteries of the sea. He realised that the village's collective secret wasn't just about Gladys; it was about their entire way of life, their relationship with the ocean that both sustained and threatened them. It was a secret born of necessity, of a primal need to survive in a place where the extraordinary was an everyday occurrence, and where the truth, when it surfaced, was often too terrifying to behold.

Unearthing Gladys' Connections

The fragmented notes, tucked away in a hidden compartment of Gladys's easel, were more than just artistic jottings; they were a map, charting a course through the labyrinthine folklore of Ballyknock. Detective O'Connell, his fingers stained with a faint, dried pigment, pieced together a narrative far removed from the image of a simple landscape artist. Gladys Quinn, it became clear, had been on a quest, a deeply personal and increasingly urgent search that had led her down paths few in Ballyknock dared to tread.

Among the sketches of wind-whipped cliffs and the tumultuous sea, O'Connell found a series of letters, their paper brittle with age, the ink faded but still legible. They were addressed to Maeve, the village elder whose words had carried such a weight of unspoken knowledge. The correspondence began innocently enough, with Gladys seeking guidance on depicting the nuances of the local dialect and the subtle shifts in the coastline's moods. But as the letters progressed, the tone shifted, the questions becoming more pointed, more insistent. Gladys was no longer asking about the aesthetics of Ballyknock; she was delving into its very soul.

"Dear Maeve," one letter read, dated just three months before Gladys's disappearance, "I find myself drawn to the stories you alluded to, the ones that aren't spoken aloud in the pubs, the tales of the 'sea-kin' and the old pacts. Your mention of the standing stones near the Embrace... could you tell me more about their significance? My research suggests a connection to something far older than the village itself."

O'Connell's brow furrowed. He recalled Maeve's cryptic pronouncements about the sea being "older than us" and demanding "respect." It seemed Gladys had picked up on these threads, pulling them with a determination that bordered on obsession. The letters continued, each one a further step into the village's guarded past. Gladys asked about specific rituals, about the timing of certain moon phases in relation to the tides, about the purpose of the carved amulets that some of the older villagers still wore, dismissed by many as mere trinkets. She was seeking a pattern, a logic within the seemingly irrational beliefs that permeated Ballyknock.

"Maeve, I've been observing the tides," another letter stated, the handwriting becoming more hurried, almost frantic. "There are days, particularly around the new moon, when the ebb and flow seem... different. Not just stronger, but with a rhythm that feels... intentional. Is this something others have noticed? Or is it just my artist's imagination playing tricks?" She enclosed a small, detailed sketch of the water's movement, a series of arrows and notations that spoke of meticulous observation. O'Connell felt a prickle of unease. He remembered Finn's hushed mention of "unnatural tides." Had Gladys witnessed the same anomaly, and had her artistic curiosity ignited something far more dangerous?

The letters revealed Gladys's growing frustration with the veil of silence that surrounded these topics. "I understand the need for discretion," she wrote, her words sharp with an edge of desperation, "but the silence feels… heavy. It's as if everyone is waiting for something. Or guarding against something. The more I try to understand, the more I feel the resistance. It's as if the village itself is trying to push me away from a truth it already knows."

But it wasn't just the correspondence with Maeve that painted a picture of a Gladys on a precipice. Tucked amongst Gladys's sketchbooks, O'Connell found a small, leather-bound diary, its pages filled with a cramped, almost illegible script. It was clearly written in haste, often in the fading light, and many of the entries were mere fragments, single words or short phrases that hinted at clandestine activities.

"Whispers by the standing stones. Not the wind."

"He waited. Moon low. Fog rolling in."

"The old symbols… they glowed?"

"He spoke of the 'deep song.' Said I needed to listen."

Who was 'he'? O'Connell sifted through the names of the few men Gladys might have known in Ballyknock. Finn, the taciturn fisherman? Liam, the young man who worked the boats? Or someone else entirely, someone from outside the village who shared her burgeoning interest in its hidden lore? The fragmented notes spoke of furtive meetings, of shared secrets under the cloak of darkness, of conversations that transgressed the boundaries of the ordinary.

One entry, scrawled with unusual urgency, sent a shiver down O'Connell's spine: "He said I was close. Too close. That some doors are meant to stay shut. But if I can just understand the ritual of the turning tides…" The sentence trailed off, unfinished, mirroring the abrupt end to Gladys's life.

O'Connell revisited the cove, the place the villagers referred to with a mixture of reverence and dread as 'the Embrace.' The standing stones, weathered and ancient, loomed against the bruised twilight sky. They seemed to hum with a latent energy, a silent testament to rituals long forgotten, or perhaps, still practiced. Gladys had been drawn to this place, a place that seemed to hold the very essence of Ballyknock's enigmatic past. Her notes suggested she had met someone here, someone who was both a guide and a warning.

He cross-referenced the dates mentioned in Gladys's diary with the village's local calendar of events, or rather, the lack thereof. Ballyknock was a place where the rhythm of life was dictated not by official holidays, but by the cycles of the moon and the sea. There were mentions of 'gatherings' near the Embrace during specific celestial alignments, events that were never publicly announced, always shrouded in secrecy. These were not the casual encounters of a curious artist; these were deliberate meetings, part of a deeper, more complex engagement with the village's hidden traditions.

O'Connell's mind raced. Gladys's fascination wasn't a superficial interest. She was actively seeking to participate, to understand, perhaps even to revive, something that the villagers had actively suppressed. Her artistic talents had provided her with an entry point, a socially acceptable reason to explore the wilder, more untamed aspects of Ballyknock. But her true objective, it seemed, was something far more profound, a connection to the ancient rites and the beliefs that lay at the heart of the community's fearful respect for the sea.

He recalled Mrs. Gable's dismissive wave of the hand when he'd mentioned Gladys's walks by the Embrace. "Artists are drawn to beauty, aren't they?" she'd said. But O'Connell now suspected that Gladys had found more than just aesthetic beauty there. She had stumbled upon a living history, a subterranean current of belief and practice that ran counter to the placid surface of village life. Her intense curiosity, her drive to uncover the truth, had made her a threat. Not a threat to the villagers' safety in the conventional sense, but a threat to their carefully maintained equilibrium, to the fragile peace they had brokered with the ancient, powerful forces that governed their lives.

The unknown individual Gladys had been meeting – was he a guardian of these traditions, or a fellow seeker? The diary entries offered conflicting clues. "He seemed to understand," read one entry, suggesting a shared pursuit. But another hinted at a darker agenda: "He warned me. Said the sea remembers everything. Said I was disturbing its rest." This duality suggested a complex relationship, one where fascination and fear were inextricably intertwined.

O'Connell's investigation had shifted from a search for a missing person to an unravelling of a carefully guarded secret. Gladys Quinn was not simply a victim of the sea; she was a participant in a drama far older than herself, a drama played out in the shadows of Ballyknock's history, a drama that the villagers, in their collective silence, were desperately trying to keep from repeating. Her connection to Maeve, her clandestine meetings, and her obsessive pursuit of local lore all pointed to a truth that was as unsettling as it was undeniable: Gladys had actively sought out the very elements that had ultimately consumed her. She had looked into the abyss, and the abyss, it seemed, had looked back, drawing her into its depths with an irresistible, ancient pull. The question now was not just what had happened to Gladys, but what had she discovered that was so dangerous, and who had been trying to stop her from revealing it? The answer, O'Connell suspected, lay buried deeper than any shipwreck, within the collective memory and the unspoken pacts of Ballyknock itself. He felt a growing certainty that Gladys's disappearance was intrinsically linked to the very traditions she had been so determined to unearth, and that the 'unknown individual' was a key player in this unfolding mystery, a player who had clearly succeeded in silencing her before she could fully understand the 'deep song' she had heard. The fragmented notes were not just clues; they were echoes of a confrontation, a desperate attempt to document a truth that was already slipping away, swallowed by the encroaching mists and the relentless rhythm of the waves.

The Old Ruins Above the Cove

The air above Cailleach's Embrace tasted of salt and something older, a primal tang that O'Connell couldn't quite place. He'd followed Gladys's almost imperceptible trail, not of footprints in the soft earth – those had long been erased by the ceaseless wind and the occasional deluge – but of a more intangible sense of her presence, a lingering echo of her obsessive quest. The path, barely more than a sheep track, snaked upwards, away from the churning maw of the cove and towards the skeletal remains of structures that defied easy explanation. They were ruins, undoubtedly, but of a kind that spoke of purpose and ritual, not mere habitation.

He reached the crest, and the full expanse of the ruins unfolded before him. Crumbling stone walls, bleached grey by sun and sea spray, formed a jagged outline against the vast, indifferent sky. Here and there, larger, more deliberate blocks of stone jutted from the earth, hinting at foundations, at a scale of construction that spoke of a community long vanished. Gladys's sketches had hinted at this place, but seeing it, feeling the palpable weight of its desolation, was something else entirely. It was a place where the veil between worlds felt thin, where the very stones seemed to absorb and retain the whispers of forgotten ages.

O'Connell moved through the scattered debris, his boots crunching on loose scree and fragments of pottery, each shard a tiny testament to lives lived and lost. He ran his gloved hand over the surface of a massive, semi-collapsed archway. The stone was pitted and worn smooth by countless seasons, but even in its decay, there was a sense of deliberate craftsmanship. The same hand, he suspected, that had carved the cryptic symbols in Gladys's journal, the ones that had so unnerved him. He scanned the ground, his eyes sharp, searching for anything that might connect this desolate place to Gladys's final days.

His gaze fell upon a low, flat stone, larger than the others, positioned almost like a forgotten altar. The surface was stained with dark, unidentifiable patches, and around its edges, the stone was subtly hollowed, as if by the repeated action of water, or perhaps, something more. He knelt, his detective's instinct kicking in, a low thrum of anticipation vibrating beneath the professional calm. The wind whipped around him, carrying with it the mournful cry of gulls and the incessant roar of the waves below, a ceaseless, elemental chorus that seemed to underscore the profound silence of the ruins themselves.

He began to examine the area more closely, his attention drawn to a series of faint indentations on the altar stone. They were weathered, almost invisible, but under the harsh light of his torch, a pattern began to emerge. It wasn't a language he recognized, nor a familiar symbol, but there was a definite intentionality to the marks, a geometry that felt ancient and profound. He recognized it instantly – the same motif that had appeared in Gladys's notebook, rendered in her delicate, precise lines, a swirl that seemed to mimic the eddying of water or the unfurling of a fern. It was here, he felt, that Gladys had found something, or someone.

He traced the outline of the carving with his finger, the rough stone a stark contrast to the smooth, almost alive quality it seemed to possess. The wind gusted, and for a fleeting moment, the air around the altar seemed to grow heavy, charged with an unseen energy. He felt a chill that had nothing to do with the temperature, a prickle of unease that crawled up his spine. This place, he realized, was not merely a collection of old stones; it was a nexus, a focal point of energies that had shaped the lives and beliefs of the people who had built it.

Moving away from the altar, O'Connell explored the perimeter of the ruins. He noticed the remains of smaller stone structures, some circular, others rectangular, their purpose lost to time. One section of the outer wall, remarkably intact, bore the faint traces of carvings that were more recognizable, though still heavily eroded. There were depictions of waves, rendered in a stylized, almost abstract manner, and what appeared to be figures, their forms indistinct, bowed in reverence or perhaps supplication. And then, he saw it. Tucked away in a small, natural recess in the stone, almost perfectly concealed by a tangle of hardy sea-grass, was something unexpected.

It was a small, leather-bound book, its cover warped and stained by the elements, but still recognizably a journal. He approached with caution, his heart hammering a little faster. This had to be it. The hidden alcove Gladys had alluded to in her notes, the one where she had found something that had so captivated her. He reached out, his fingers brushing against the rough, weathered surface of the leather. It felt ancient, imbued with a history that predated even these crumbling stones.

Carefully, he extracted the journal from its hiding place. The leather was brittle, and he handled it with the utmost delicacy, fearful of causing further damage. He opened it, and the smell of old paper and sea-dampened ink filled his nostrils. The pages were filled with writing, in a faded, elegant script that he recognized as Gladys's, but different from the hurried, almost frantic entries in the diary found amongst her belongings. This script was more deliberate, more focused, as if she had found a quiet place to record her discoveries.

The entries spoke of rituals, of offerings made to the sea, of an ancient pact between the people of this place and the ocean itself. Gladys detailed her attempts to decipher the carvings on the altar stone, her growing understanding of the symbols, and her fascination with the recurring motif of the swirl, which she believed represented the 'heartbeat' of the sea. One entry, dated only a few weeks before her disappearance, sent a jolt of cold dread through him.

"The carvings speak of appeasement," she had written, her script still legible despite the fading ink. "A pact made in the deep past, to ensure the bounty of the sea, but also to curb its wrath. The cycle must be maintained. The old ways must be honored." She described her efforts to replicate the rituals, her growing conviction that the sea was not a passive entity, but one that demanded respect, and indeed, active engagement.

Another passage detailed a specific ceremony, tied to the lunar cycle and the ebb and flow of the tides. "The turning of the tide, not merely a physical phenomenon, but a spiritual one," she wrote. "A moment of balance, when the boundary between worlds is thinnest. The offering must be made then, a symbol of surrender, a plea for continued favor." The journal also contained sketches of intricately woven objects, made from dried seaweed and driftwood, and of small, polished stones inscribed with the familiar swirling pattern. These, she believed, were the tokens of appeasement.

O'Connell flipped through the pages, his gaze snagging on a particularly poignant entry, a desperate plea that seemed to echo the very heart of the village's unspoken fears. "The sea is restless," Gladys had written, her handwriting betraying a growing anxiety. "It remembers the broken promises. The old pact is weakening. We must find a way to renew it, to appease the deep currents before they overwhelm us. If the balance is lost... the consequences will be terrible."

He looked up from the journal, his mind reeling. This was not just artistic curiosity; this was a descent into a belief system that was as ancient as it was potent. Gladys had stumbled upon something that the villagers had long sought to bury, a forgotten history that still held sway over their lives. The fragmented notes, the cryptic conversations, the veiled warnings – they all pointed to this place, to these rituals, to this ancient pact.

He noticed a small, circular indentation on the altar stone, perfectly sized to hold one of the carved stones Gladys had sketched. He looked around the immediate vicinity, sifting through the loose soil and debris. His fingers closed around something smooth and cool. It was a stone, worn smooth by the sea, and on its surface, the familiar, swirling pattern was faintly visible, a testament to Gladys's efforts, or perhaps, to the efforts of those who had come before her.

He then noticed a small, almost invisible seam in the rock face behind the altar. Running his fingers along it, he felt a slight give. He pushed, and a section of the stone, no larger than his hand, swung inward, revealing a small, dark cavity. Inside, nestled on a bed of dried kelp, was a single, tarnished silver locket. He picked it up, his hand trembling slightly. It was intricately engraved, the swirling motif repeated on its surface. He opened it. Inside, on one side, was a faded miniature portrait of a woman, her features indistinct but her eyes holding a profound sadness. On the other side, a single, stark word was inscribed: "Balance."

O'Connell felt a profound sense of melancholy wash over him. Gladys had been searching for balance, for understanding, for a way to connect with something that was slipping away. Her journal here, in this desolate place, spoke of a deep understanding of the village's underlying anxieties, of the unspoken pact that governed their relationship with the sea. She had uncovered not just folklore, but a living, breathing tradition, a set of beliefs that were deeply ingrained in the very fabric of Ballyknock.

He carefully placed the locket back in the alcove, and then, with immense care, closed the stone panel. This discovery felt too significant, too sensitive, to be disturbed further without proper consideration. He looked out at the vast, unforgiving expanse of the sea, its surface a deceptive mirror of the sky. He understood now why the villagers were so reticent, so guarded. They lived in the shadow of an ancient power, a power that demanded respect, appeasement, and a constant vigilance.

Gladys, in her quest for truth, had stepped too close to that power, and in doing so, had perhaps disrupted the delicate, centuries-old balance. Her journal was not just a record of her discoveries, but a testament to her growing fear, a fear that was now mirrored in his own. The ruins above Cailleach's Embrace held secrets, yes, but they also held a warning, a chilling echo of a pact that was as binding as it was terrifying. He had found the place, and he had found Gladys's testament, but the ultimate mystery – what had happened to her, and why – remained shrouded in the mist and the timeless roar of the sea. The journal was a key, but it unlocked a door to a history far more complex and dangerous than he had ever imagined, a history that the villagers had spent generations trying to forget, or perhaps, trying to keep hidden from themselves.

CHAPTER FOUR — THE UNSEEN HAND

The Stranger in the Village

The wind, a constant, mournful companion on this desolate coast, whipped O'Connell's coat around him as he descended from the ruins above Cailleach's Embrace. The weight of Gladys's journal, tucked securely inside his own oilskin, felt heavier than its physical mass suggested. He'd found the nexus she'd written about, the place where the ancient pacts were etched into stone and whispered by the sea. He'd found her last testament, a chronicle of her descent into the village's most guarded secrets, a descent that had clearly culminated in a profound and terrible fear. But the central question remained unanswered, a gaping hole in the narrative of her disappearance: who else knew? And more importantly, who else had been watching?

His thoughts, a tangled skein of Gladys's cryptic words and the stark reality of the ruins, turned to Finn. The old fisherman, his face a roadmap of weathered lines, had been the first to mention an anomaly, a ripple in the predictable tide of Ballyknock's existence. Finn's words, initially dismissed as the ramblings of an old man touched by the sea's solitude, now resonated with an unnerving prescience. He'd spoken of a stranger, a man who didn't belong, someone who moved with a quiet purpose that set him apart from the familiar rhythms of village life. O'Connell had initially focused on the tangible evidence, the ruins, the journal, the locket. Now, he needed to delve into the intangible, the whispers and rumours that formed the true fabric of a secluded community.

He made his way back towards the village, the salty air doing little to clear the fog of unease that had settled upon him. The path wound through sparse, wind-blasted heather, the only sounds the cry of the gulls and the ceaseless percussion of the waves against the rocky shore. He pictured Finn's hands, gnarled and strong, as he'd recounted his sighting. "Just passin' through," Finn had said, his voice raspy. "But he weren't like the summer folk, nor the hikers. Had a look about him, like he was searchin' for somethin' specific. Asked me about the old cove, he did. The one the women warned us about." Finn had squinted out towards the sea, his gaze distant. "Said he was interested in the local lore. But his questions… they were too sharp, ye know? Not like a curious tourist. More like… like he knew what he was lookin' for."

O'Connell resolved to speak to Finn again, but discreetly. The villagers of Ballyknock, he'd already learned, were a tight-lipped bunch, their loyalty fiercely guarded, their secrets buried deep. Direct questioning would likely yield nothing but polite evasion or outright suspicion. He needed to approach this like a fisherman mending his nets, patiently untangling the threads, piecing together the fragments.

His first stop was the small, dimly lit pub at the heart of the village, The Salty Siren. The air inside was thick with the smell of peat smoke, stale ale, and the faint, lingering scent of fish. A few of the local men, their faces weathered and tanned, sat nursing their drinks, their conversation a low murmur that ceased abruptly as O'Connell entered. He caught the flicker of curiosity in their eyes, the quick, assessing glances that spoke volumes. He ordered a pint of Guinness, the familiar ritual a small anchor in the sea of uncertainty.

He found a quiet corner, nursing his drink and observing. The faces were familiar from his brief time in Ballyknock, etched with the hardships and isolation of their lives. He needed to find someone who might have seen this stranger, someone who wasn't as wary as the others. His gaze fell upon Liam, a younger man, perhaps in his late twenties, who worked as a deckhand on one of the fishing boats. Liam seemed more approachable, less ingrained in the village's older, more ingrained reticence.

O'Connell casually drifted over to Liam's table. "Evening," he said, offering a friendly nod. "Quiet night."

Liam grunted in response, his eyes still fixed on the scarred surface of the wooden table. "Always quiet, this time o' year."

"Just wondering," O'Connell began, choosing his words carefully, "if you've seen any new faces around lately? Any tourists or anything?"

Liam finally looked up, his gaze guarded. "Few enough. Hikers sometimes. They stick to the main paths, though." He paused, then added, almost reluctantly, "There was one other, though. A few days back. Didn't see him myself, but young Tommy O'Malley mentioned him. Said he saw a fella wanderin' down towards the cove path. Didn't look like he was aimin' for a stroll."

"Towards the cove?" O'Connell's interest piqued. "What did he look like?"

Liam shrugged, his disinterest feigned. "Tommy said he was tall. Dark clothes. Had a way about him, Tommy said. Like he was… watchin'. Not friendly-like." He took a long drink of his beer, his eyes darting towards the other patrons, as if gauging their reaction. "Tommy said he asked him about the path, if it led anywhere in particular. When Tommy said it just went to the old ruins, the fella just nodded, like he already knew."

O'Connell felt a subtle shift, a confirmation of Finn's account. This stranger wasn't just a passing observer; he was actively seeking information, and his interest lay squarely in the area O'Connell was investigating. "Did he say anything else?" O'Connell pressed, keeping his tone casual. "Where he was from, what he was doing?"

"Nah," Liam said, shaking his head. "Tommy reckoned he was a city fella. Too clean, too… sharp. Like he didn't belong in the salt and spray of it all." He hesitated, then lowered his voice slightly. "Said the fella asked about the name of the cove, too. And… and if anyone had been seen near it lately."

O'Connell's mind raced. The cove. The ruins. The questions about recent activity. It all pointed to a deliberate investigation, an outsider with an agenda that seemed to intersect directly with Gladys's own journey. He needed more. He decided to seek out Tommy O'Malley himself.

He found Tommy down by the harbour, helping his father mend fishing nets. The boy, no older than fifteen, was wiry and quick-eyed, his face still bearing the softness of youth. O'Connell approached him, offering a small, encouraging smile.

"Tommy, isn't it?" O'Connell said, his voice gentle. "Liam mentioned you saw someone unusual the other day."

Tommy's eyes widened slightly, a flicker of apprehension crossing his face. He glanced at his father, who offered a subtle, almost imperceptible nod. "Aye," Tommy replied, his voice hesitant. "Saw a man on the path to the cove. He was walking towards it, not away."

"And he asked you about the path?" O'Connell prompted.

"Aye. He asked if it was a safe walk. I said it was rough. He just nodded and kept goin'. Then he turned back and asked if I knew the cove's name. Said he'd heard it called... uh... Cailleach's Embrace." Tommy's voice dropped to a near whisper on the last phrase, a hint of the local superstition touching his young voice.

"And what did you say?" O'Connell asked, his gaze steady.

"I said aye. And he asked if anyone went there often. I said no, not usually. Not for a long time." Tommy fiddled with a strand of netting. "Then he asked if I'd seen anyone else around there. Anyone... looking for something."

O'Connell felt a chill seep into his bones, colder than the sea breeze. That was it. The stranger wasn't just asking about the cove; he was asking about Gladys, or at least, about someone else who had been drawn to this place. "And had you?" O'Connell asked, his voice carefully neutral. "Seen anyone?"

Tommy's gaze drifted towards the wild, windswept headland where the ruins lay. "Well," he mumbled, his voice barely audible, "there was a woman. A few weeks ago. Came down this way a fair bit. Carried a sketchbook."

O'Connell's breath hitched. Gladys. The stranger had been asking about her. "A woman," he repeated, his mind already piecing together the timeline. "Did you speak to her?"

Tommy shook his head. "No. She mostly kept to herself. But she looked... very interested in the stones up there. Saw her drawing them." He looked directly at O'Connell, his young face earnest. "She looked... like she was trying to understand something. Something important."

The stranger, asking about the cove, about people looking for something, and Gladys being seen there, sketching the stones. The pieces were falling into place, forming a disturbing mosaic of external interest in Ballyknock's most guarded secret. This stranger, this outsider, had arrived at a critical juncture, a time when Gladys was deepening her investigation, when the village's ancient pacts were becoming her obsession.

"Did this man," O'Connell asked, leaning closer, "did he mention anything else? His name, perhaps?"

Tommy's brow furrowed in thought. "No. But he had these... eyes. Very intense. Like he could see right through you. And he had a strange way of talkin'. Not like us. Too... precise." He paused, as if trying to recall a detail. "He was carrying a small bag, too. Dark leather. Looked expensive."

Expensive. Precise. Intense gaze. Asking about the cove, about Gladys, about people "looking for something." O'Connell felt a growing certainty that this stranger was not a casual tourist. He was someone with a specific purpose, someone who might be connected to Gladys's disappearance in a far more direct and sinister way than he had initially feared.

He thanked Tommy and left the harbour, his mind buzzing. The encounter with the stranger, however brief and anecdotal, felt like a pivotal moment. It suggested an external force at play, someone who might have been observing Gladys, perhaps even influencing her. Had he been the one who alerted her to something? Or was he the reason she had disappeared?

O'Connell decided to return to Finn. The old fisherman, with his keen eyes and intimate knowledge of the village and its inhabitants, was his best source. He found Finn mending his lobster pots near the small, weathered pier. The rhythmic clinking of the metal rings and the smell of brine filled the air.

"Finn," O'Connell said, approaching him respectfully. "A moment of your time?"

Finn looked up, his weathered face creased in a friendly but wary expression. "O'Connell. Back from your walk?"

"Indeed," O'Connell replied, sitting on a nearby overturned crate. "I was thinking about what you said earlier, about seeing a stranger."

Finn grunted, his hands continuing their work. "Aye, the one with the sharp eyes."

"Tommy O'Malley saw him too," O'Connell continued. "He asked Tommy about the cove, and if anyone had been seen there recently, looking for something."

Finn's work paused for a beat. His eyes, usually twinkling with a certain mischievousness, narrowed with a more serious, assessing look. "Did he now?"

"Yes," O'Connell confirmed. "And Tommy mentioned the stranger seemed very interested in the cove's name, and in whether anyone had been seen exploring the ruins." He watched Finn closely. "It makes me wonder, Finn, if this man wasn't just a curious traveler. Do you think he might have had a particular interest in Gladys Burton?"

Finn finally set down his tools. He stared out at the restless sea, his gaze distant, thoughtful. The silence stretched, punctuated only by the cries of the gulls and the distant rumble of the waves. When he finally spoke, his voice was low, almost a murmur. "Gladys… she was a bright spark, that one. Too bright for her own good, maybe. Always asking questions, diggin' where she shouldn't. That cove… it's always held a pull for those who want to understand. But understand what? That's the question."

He turned back to O'Connell, his expression unreadable. "This stranger… if he was askin' about the cove and about people searchin'… it could be nothing. Or it could be everything." He sighed, a deep, weary sound. "There are those who want the old ways to stay buried, O'Connell. And there are those who want to dig them up. Sometimes, those two groups cross paths."

"And this stranger?" O'Connell pressed. "Did he seem like he wanted them buried, or dug up?"

Finn scratched his grizzled chin. "Hard to say. He had a… an edge to him. Like a hawk watchin' a mouse. Not predatory, exactly, but watchful. Like he knew the game that was being played, and he was playing his own part." He paused, his gaze sweeping over the scattered houses of Ballyknock. "There's old families here, O'Connell. Families with long memories and long traditions. They don't take kindly to outsiders pokin' around. Especially not when it comes to the sea. The sea… it demands respect. And it keeps its own counsel."

O'Connell understood. The village was a tightly woven tapestry of history, belief, and deep-seated tradition. Gladys, in her pursuit of the past, had inadvertently stepped into a world that many in Ballyknock actively sought to keep hidden, a world that this stranger now seemed to be a part of. His questions weren't just idle curiosity; they were probing, targeted inquiries that suggested he was following a similar path to Gladys's, or perhaps, actively trying to intercept her.

"Did anyone else see him, Finn?" O'Connell asked, his voice hushed. "Anyone who might know more?"

Finn hesitated, his gaze drifting towards the distant, mist-shrouded headland. "Old Mrs. Doyle, up the hill. She sees more from her cottage window than any of us realize. She's a bit… eccentric, but her eyes are sharp enough. She mentioned a car, parked unusual-like, a few days back. Not one of ours, she said. Too sleek. Too quiet."

A sleek, quiet car. It fit the profile of an outsider, someone who could move through Ballyknock without drawing undue attention, yet leave a distinct impression. O'Connell filed the information away. Mrs. Doyle would be his next stop. He needed to understand how deeply this stranger's presence had resonated within the village, and whether his inquiries had been noted by more than just the younger generation.

As he walked away from the pier, the image of Gladys's journal, with its increasingly frantic entries about the sea's restlessness and the weakening of the pact, solidified in his mind. The stranger's appearance, coinciding with Gladys's heightened interest in the cove, felt less like a coincidence and more like a deliberate convergence. Had he been an adversary, seeking to silence Gladys? Or had he been an ally, drawn to Ballyknock by the same ancient secrets that had captivated her? The intensity of his gaze, the precision of his questions, suggested a purpose far beyond that of a mere academic interest. He was an unseen hand, reaching into the heart of Ballyknock's deepest mysteries, and O'Connell feared that hand might have been the one to push Gladys into the unforgiving embrace of the sea. The puzzle of her disappearance had just gained a new, unsettling dimension, and the shadow of this unknown figure now loomed large over the windswept shores of Ballyknock. He had to find this stranger, for he suspected the stranger held a key to Gladys's fate, a key forged in the ancient whispers of the cove and the turbulent currents of the past.

The Significance of the Camera

The salt-laced wind seemed to whisper secrets O'Connell couldn't quite decipher as he replayed the meager findings from Gladys's camera. It was a small, rugged thing, designed for durability, not elegance, its lens coated in a fine sheen of sea spray that mirrored the perpetual dampness of Ballyknock. The memory card, when he'd first retrieved it from the satchel he'd found near the cliffs, had been frustratingly formatted. Not completely wiped, not entirely clean, but a chaotic jumble of deleted files and corrupted data, as if someone had tried to be thorough, but perhaps not entirely successful. He'd sent it to a contact in the city, a wizard with pixels and data streams named Anya, known for her ability to coax ghosts from dead drives.

Anya's initial report had been terse, as always: "Fragmented. Significant damage. Some recovery possible, but expect gaps. Large gaps." O'Connell had understood. Gladys's camera, like her journal, was a record of her descent, and it seemed this descent had been meticulously, if imperfectly, documented. The recovery process had been painstaking, a digital archaeology of sorts, sifting through the digital detritus for any meaningful trace.

The first recovered images were, as expected, of the landscape. Not the postcard-perfect vistas of tourist brochures, but stark, unvarnished views of Ballyknock and its surroundings. Gladys had a keen eye for the raw, untamed beauty of the place. There were shots of the weathered cottages huddled against the relentless wind, the churning grey sea meeting the jagged cliffs, and the desolate, windswept moors. These were interspersed with close-ups of ancient standing stones, their surfaces eroded by centuries of wind and rain, moss clinging to their crevices like ancient skin. They were powerful images, imbued with a sense of timelessness, but they offered no immediate clues to her fate.

Then came the fragments of the stranger. Anya had managed to stitch together a few stills, pixelated and blurry, but undeniably depicting the man Finn and Tommy had described. Tall, clad in dark, nondescript clothing that seemed to absorb the meager light. His face was often obscured, turned away from the lens, or caught in a profile that revealed little. Yet, there was an intensity to his posture, an almost predatory stillness that O'Connell recognized from his own observations of the world. One image, particularly striking, showed the man standing at the edge of the cliffs, his back to the camera, gazing out at the turbulent sea. He appeared utterly alone, yet his stance suggested a connection to the very elements that surrounded him, as if he were a part of the wild landscape rather than merely passing through it. It was the same unnerving stillness that Finn had described, the sense of a man who didn't belong, but who was nonetheless deeply engaged with his surroundings.

O'Connell zoomed in on the image, trying to discern any detail in the man's silhouette. The dark clothing seemed expensive, the cut of his jacket suggesting a tailored garment rather than off-the-rack. He held a small, dark object in his hand, its purpose indistinguishable in the low resolution. Anya's annotations indicated that this object had been the target of a deliberate attempt to corrupt the data surrounding it. Someone had wanted that particular detail scrubbed.

The fragmented video clips were even more tantalizing, and ultimately, more disturbing. They were short, jerky, and interspersed with static and the maddening hiss of corrupted audio. The first few were of the ruins Gladys had visited, her voice, tinny and slightly distorted, narrating her observations about the strange markings on the stones. O'Connell could hear the growing excitement in her tone, the thrill of discovery that had always driven her. She spoke of a pattern, a language etched into the very fabric of the place, a connection to the sea that felt both ancient and alive.

But it was the last recovered clip that sent a cold dread through O'Connell. It was shaky, clearly shot in haste, and the audio was a chaotic blend of wind, waves, and what sounded like distant voices. The visual was Gladys's own perspective, her hand holding the camera steady for a moment before it began to waver. She was near the cove, the jagged rocks of Cailleach's Embrace looming in the background. The light was fading, casting long, distorted shadows.

Gladys's voice, barely a whisper, was audible above the din. "It's… it's not just stone," she breathed, the awe palpable.

Then, a sudden sharp intake of breath. The camera lurched violently, as if she had been startled or pushed. For a fleeting moment, a figure appeared in the periphery of the frame – the stranger, his face illuminated by a brief, unnatural flash of light. He seemed to be reaching out, or perhaps blocking her path. Gladys's gasp was sharp, terrified, and then the camera spun wildly, the image dissolving into a blur of light and shadow. The audio cut off abruptly, leaving only the overwhelming roar of the sea.

O'Connell felt a physical jolt. This wasn't just about historical inquiry anymore; it was about a direct confrontation. Gladys had seen him, been seen by him, and in that final, terrifying moment, it seemed he had intervened. The fragmented images and the single, chilling video clip painted a picture of a calculated intrusion into Gladys's investigation. The stranger wasn't just observing; he was actively involved, and his involvement had coincided with Gladys's most profound discoveries.

He stared at the screen, the recovered images flickering before his eyes. The meticulous attempt to erase the data related to the stranger, the final desperate moments captured on Gladys's camera – it all pointed to a deliberate effort to silence her, or at the very least, to stop her from revealing whatever truth she had uncovered. The implications were chilling. This wasn't just a lost hiker or an amateur historian. This was someone with a vested interest in keeping Ballyknock's secrets buried, someone who was willing to take extreme measures.

He thought back to Finn's words: "He had a look about him, like he was searchin' for somethin' specific." And Tommy's observation: "Said the fella asked about the name of the cove, too. And… and if anyone had been seen near it lately." These weren't the questions of a tourist. They were the questions of an investigator, or perhaps, a hunter. And Gladys, with her insatiable curiosity and her uncanny ability to unearth hidden truths, had become his quarry.

The fact that Gladys had been filming, even in those final moments, suggested she had anticipated danger, or at least, had a premonition of something significant about to happen. She was documenting her findings, perhaps intending to share them, to make sure her work wouldn't be lost. But the partial wiping of the memory card spoke of a desperate, last-minute attempt to conceal something, or to prevent it from being seen. Had Gladys herself tried to wipe it before she was… interrupted? Or had the stranger done it, with a misguided attempt at thoroughness?

O'Connell leaned back, the weight of the new information pressing down on him. The stranger was no longer an abstract possibility; he was a tangible presence, a central figure in the unfolding tragedy. His connection to Gladys's disappearance was now undeniable, a dark thread woven through the fabric of her final days. The mystery had deepened, its tendrils reaching out from the ancient stones and the whispering sea, now clearly ensnared by an external force, a force that had clearly been watching, waiting, and finally, acting. The significance of the camera, and the fragmented story it told, was immense. It confirmed that Gladys had been on the verge of a breakthrough, and that someone had gone to great lengths to ensure that breakthrough never saw the light of day. He needed to find out who this stranger was, and what ancient secrets he was so desperately trying to protect, or perhaps, to exploit. The recovered fragments were not answers, but they were a powerful new set of questions, each one more urgent than the last. He looked out at the relentless, grey sea, feeling a profound sense of urgency. Gladys had found something, and someone had ensured she would never tell. The unseen hand had made its move.

The Fisherman's Secret

O'Connell found Finn mending a tangled net on the quay, his movements slow and deliberate, like a ritual. The afternoon sun, a watery disc behind the perpetual Ballyknock haze, glinted off the brine-soaked twine. The air still carried the sharp tang of the sea, mingled with the less pleasant aroma of drying fish. O'Connell approached, the crunch of his boots on the scattered pebbles a stark contrast to the rhythmic scraping of Finn's knife.

"Finn," O'Connell began, his voice low, cutting through the drone of the gulls. "We need to talk. About Gladys."

Finn paused, his weathered hands stilling, though he didn't look up immediately. The silence stretched, thick with unspoken things. Finally, he met O'Connell's gaze, his blue eyes, usually as clear and direct as the sea on a calm day, now clouded with a familiar reticence. "Aye, Detective. What more is there to say?"

"More than you've told me," O'Connell replied, stepping closer. "I know she spoke with you. I know you saw her, more than once. And I know you saw the man." He let the words hang in the air, observing Finn's reaction. The fisherman's face, a roadmap of a life lived at sea, tightened almost imperceptibly around the eyes.

"She was a curious lass," Finn said, his voice raspy, turning back to the net. "Too curious for her own good, I reckon."

"Curious about what, Finn?" O'Connell pressed, his tone unwavering. "What did she find that frightened you so much you felt the need to warn her off?"

Finn sighed, a sound like the wind whistling through a ship's rigging. He put down his knife and straightened up, running a calloused hand over his greying beard. The weariness in his posture was profound, etched deeper than the lines on his face. "It's not somethin' we talk about, Detective. Not openly. It's... tradition. Old ways."

"Tradition," O'Connell echoed, the word tasting strange on his tongue. "Gladys was a historian, Finn. Her life was about uncovering old ways, understanding them. Why would you try to stop her from understanding something that's part of this village's history?"

"Because some things," Finn said, his gaze drifting towards the restless sea, "are best left undisturbed. She was askin' about... the offerings. The old appeasements."

O'Connell felt a prickle of ice run down his spine. Offerings? Appeasements? This was no longer just about historical research. "Offerings to whom, Finn? For what?"

"To the sea," Finn said simply, as if stating the obvious. "For good catches. For safe passage. For... the bounty. Been done for generations, by a few families. A quiet thing, you understand. Not for show. Just... a way of keepin' the balance."

"And Gladys stumbled upon this balance?"

Finn nodded slowly. "She'd been down by Cailleach's Embrace, hadn't she? Spent a good deal of time there, pokin' around the stones. Asked a lot of questions. About the markings. About the carvings. Said they looked like prayers. Or pleas." He gave a short, bitter laugh. "More like instructions, I told her. Instructions on how to keep the sea happy."

"And you warned her?"

"Aye. I told her to be careful. Told her she was stirrin' up things best left buried. Told her the elders, the families that still hold to the old ways, they wouldn't take kindly to an outsider diggin' into their business. They're a watchful lot, the elders. Protective."

"Protective of what, Finn? Of a few old stories? Or something more?" O'Connell watched Finn's face intently. There was more than just adherence to tradition in the fisherman's eyes; there was a fear, a deep-seated apprehension.

"It's about respect, Detective," Finn said, his voice taking on a more serious tone. "Respect for what the sea gives, and what it can take. Gladys, she saw it as history. Fascinatin' history, no doubt. But she didn't understand the… the living part of it. The ongoing commitment. The families, they still believe. They still practice. And they're not goin' to let anyone, least of all an outsider, disrupt that. Especially if she was startin' to uncover too much."

"What do you mean, 'too much'?" O'Connell's mind flashed back to the stranger, to the carefully corrupted data, to Gladys's terrified gasp. "Was she getting close to something the elders wanted to keep hidden?"

Finn hesitated, his gaze flicking out towards the horizon as if seeking guidance from the endless expanse of water. "She was askin' about the rituals. The specifics. The times of year. The… ingredients, you could call 'em. The old ways have their own language, Detective. And Gladys, she was learnin' it too fast."

"And the stranger?" O'Connell pushed, sensing Finn was holding back more. "Did he know about this tradition?"

Finn's jaw tightened. He picked up his knife again, but his hands trembled slightly. "He was watchin'. He wasn't from around here, that much was plain. Asked about the old families. Asked about who still… tended to the old ways. Asked about the cove."

"He asked about the cove specifically?"

"Aye. And about anyone seen near it. Said he was a researcher, lookin' into local folklore. Sounded plausible enough, I suppose. But there was somethin' about him. A hardness. Like a man who's used to takin' what he wants, not askin' for it. I didn't like the look of him, Detective. Not one bit."

"So you warned Gladys about the traditions, and the stranger was inquiring about them too. It sounds like they were both interested in the same thing, Finn, but with very different intentions."

"Perhaps," Finn conceded, his voice barely a whisper. "But Gladys… she had a good heart. She was just curious. Wanted to understand. The other one… I don't know what he wanted. But it weren't for simple understandin'."

"Did Gladys mention the stranger to you? Did she seem afraid of him?"

Finn shook his head. "She mentioned seein' a visitor. Said he was… intense. Asked her if she was one of the families involved in the old ways. She told him she was just a historian. Said he didn't seem to believe her. Said he lingered. Watched her." He paused, his eyes fixed on O'Connell. "I told her to stick to the archives, to the published histories. Told her the real stories were often buried deep, and not always safe to uncover. I told her if she kept diggin' into the traditions, she might find more than she bargained for."

"And she didn't listen?"

"She listened, aye. But she also saw the respect in the eyes of the women who still left their offerings on the shore. She saw the quiet pride in the men who spoke of the sea's generosity. She wanted to understand the

why behind it all. Not just the *what*. And that's where she started to get too close, I reckon." Finn's voice was heavy with regret. "The elders, they're not violent men, not by nature. But they're fiercely protective of their way of life. And when they see that way of life threatened, well... things can happen."

"What kind of things, Finn?" O'Connell's gaze was sharp, piercing. He knew he was close to something, a hidden current running beneath the placid surface of Ballyknock's community.

Finn looked down at his hands, his knuckles white against the rough twine. "It's not a matter of violence, not usually. It's about... discouragement. Making someone feel unwelcome. Making them feel they've made a mistake. Or, if that doesn't work..." He trailed off, unable to articulate the darker possibilities.

"Or if that doesn't work, they make them disappear?" O'Connell finished, his voice low and dangerous.

Finn flinched. "I didn't say that, Detective."

"But you thought it, didn't you?" O'Connell stepped closer, his voice a low growl. "You saw Gladys getting too close, and you saw the stranger watching her. You saw them both circling the same secret, the same tradition. And you felt you had to warn her. Because you knew, deep down, that this wasn't just about folklore. This was about power. And control. And that for some people, that secret was worth protecting at any cost."

Finn remained silent, his gaze fixed on the net, his shoulders hunched as if bearing an unbearable weight. The silence was an admission, a confession in its own right. He had tried to protect Gladys, in his own way, by warning her away. But his warnings had been for naught, lost in her relentless pursuit of the truth, a truth that, it seemed, some in Ballyknock were determined to keep buried forever. The fisherman's secret, passed down through generations, was becoming a dangerous enigma, one that had drawn Gladys, and now O'Connell, into its shadowy depths. The 'unseen hand' wasn't just the stranger; it was the weight of tradition, the fear of change, and the fierce, unyielding loyalty of a community bound by ancient pacts.

Maeves Hesitation and Hidden Truths

O'Connell found Maeve in her usual sanctuary, the small, cluttered study at the back of the library. The scent of old paper and dried herbs hung in the air, a comforting aroma that always seemed to cling to her. Sunlight, filtered through the dusty panes of the window, illuminated motes of dust dancing in the quiet air. She was hunched over a faded, leather-bound tome, her brow furrowed in concentration, a magnifying glass held steady in her hand. O'Connell's arrival, marked by the soft creak of the floorboards, didn't immediately break her focus. He waited, the weight of his recent conversation with Finn still heavy on his mind, the fisherman's veiled warnings echoing in his ears.

Finally, he cleared his throat. "Maeve."

She looked up, her eyes, the colour of sea-washed pebbles, widening slightly in surprise, then settling into a look of weary resignation. "Detective. I'd almost forgotten you were due back." Her voice was soft, tinged with the same fatigue that seemed to permeate the very walls of the old building. "Come to press me again?"

O'Connell approached her desk, placing the small, canvas evidence bag on its surface. Inside, glinting dully, were fragments of pottery and a few brittle, yellowed pages of Gladys's research, carefully preserved. "I've been at the ruins, Maeve. And I've been looking at Gladys's notes again. The ones she'd painstakingly transcribed before…" He let the sentence trail off, his gaze meeting hers. He saw a flicker of something in her eyes – apprehension, perhaps, or a deeper, more unsettling recognition.

"And you believe I have answers, Detective?" she asked, her tone carefully neutral. She pushed the magnifying glass aside, her long, slender fingers tracing the embossed pattern on the ancient book's cover.

"I believe you know more than you've told me," O'Connell stated, his voice calm but firm. "Finn alluded to 'traditions,' to 'old ways' that Gladys was delving into. He mentioned her fascination with the markings at Cailleach's Embrace, with the carvings that looked like 'prayers' or 'pleas.' He also said she was asking about 'offerings,' about 'appeasements' to the sea. He said she was learning the 'language' of these ways too quickly, and that some people wouldn't like it."

Maeve was silent for a long moment, her gaze fixed on the scattered contents of the evidence bag. Her breathing seemed to shallow. "Finn is a good man," she finally said, her voice barely audible. "He means well. But he fears what he doesn't understand, or what he believes is best left buried."

"And what do you believe, Maeve?" O'Connell pressed, leaning forward slightly. "Is this simply a matter of folklore, a few quaint rituals passed down through generations? Or is there something more to these 'appeasements'?"

Maeve finally met his gaze, and O'Connell saw a deep, profound sadness in her eyes, a sadness that seemed to stretch back centuries. She sighed, a soft, sorrowful sound. "The legend of the sacrificed priestess, Detective," she began, her voice low and carefully measured, "it's more than just a story told to frighten children or to explain the sea's moods. For centuries, it was a… a representation. A symbolic shorthand for a practice that continued, in secret, for generations."

O'Connell felt a chill, a prickle of unease that had nothing to do with the damp air of Ballyknock. "A practice? What kind of practice?"

"A ritualistic practice," Maeve explained, choosing her words with the precision of a surgeon. "One that involved… offerings. Sacrifices, in a sense, though not always in the way one might imagine. It was about appeasing the elements, about ensuring bounty, about maintaining a balance with the sea, which has always been the lifeblood of this community. And like many ancient practices, it evolved. It became less visible, more internalized, passed down within certain families, the keepers of the old ways."

"Finn mentioned these families," O'Connell said, remembering the fisherman's guarded words. "He said they were protective. He said Gladys was stirring things up that they wouldn't take kindly to."

Maeve nodded slowly, her fingers now absently turning a smooth, grey stone that lay amongst Gladys's notes. "Gladys was fascinated, as you know. Her historical curiosity was boundless. She saw the carvings, the offerings left on the shore – the small, intricately woven effigies, the handfuls of grain, the smoothed stones polished by generations of touch – not as remnants of a forgotten past, but as living traditions. She wanted to understand the context, the motivations, the *why* behind them. And she was very good at it. She was uncovering the connections, the lineage of these practices."

"And that frightened them?" O'Connell asked, picturing the tight-lipped faces of some of the older villagers he'd encountered.

"It threatened to expose something that was meant to remain private," Maeve admitted. "These traditions, they're woven into the fabric of certain families, into their identity. To have an outsider, even one as well-intentioned as Gladys, delving into their most sacred, most hidden practices… it was seen as an intrusion. A potential desecration, perhaps. Finn, he tried to warn her, to steer her towards the safer, academic routes of her research. He saw the danger."

"The danger of what, exactly?" O'Connell prompted, his mind flashing back to the stranger, the man who had been watching Gladys, asking about the old families. "Finn mentioned a stranger. Someone who was also inquiring about these traditions."

Maeve's expression tightened, a shadow crossing her face. "Ah, him." She took a deep, shaky breath. "He was… a complication. A discordant note in the symphony of Ballyknock's hidden history. He wasn't an outsider in the same way Gladys was. He was a descendant, you see. Of one of the families who traditionally uphold these practices. But he was…

estranged. Disgruntled. He believed these traditions were being diluted, perhaps even that they were being exploited by the current keepers. Or maybe he simply wanted to claim them for himself."

"Exploit or expose?" O'Connell mused, the pieces clicking into place. "So he wasn't a historian like Gladys. He was more of an opportunist, or a rebel within the system."

"Precisely," Maeve confirmed. "He saw Gladys's research, her digging into the past, as an opportunity. Perhaps he thought she could be a pawn, a tool to either expose the families he felt had wronged him, or to lend credence to his own claims. He approached her, I believe, under the guise of shared interest, a fellow scholar of local lore. But his intentions were far more… self-serving. And manipulative."

"Did Gladys tell you about him?" O'Connell asked. "Did she mention his name?"

Maeve hesitated, her gaze falling to her hands again. "She mentioned a man who seemed overly interested in her work. Someone who made her feel uneasy. She said he asked probing questions, questions that went beyond mere academic curiosity. He wanted to know about the specifics of the rituals, about the lineage, about who still practiced them actively. He was looking for leverage, Detective, not for understanding. Gladys, bless her, was too trusting. She thought his intensity was born of passion, of a shared dedication to uncovering the truth."

"And you grew fearful when she became too deeply entangled?" O'Connell repeated, recalling Finn's words about Gladys getting too close.

Maeve nodded, her eyes now glistening with unshed tears. "When I realised she was not only delving into the academic history, but was also being courted by someone with such a volatile agenda… yes, I grew afraid. I tried to advise her, to steer her away from direct confrontation with those families, to caution her about the stranger's intentions. I told her that some truths, when unearthed without proper respect or understanding, can be dangerous. That they can attract the wrong kind of attention, the kind that seeks to control rather than to preserve."

She looked directly at O'Connell, her gaze piercing. "Gladys saw these traditions as a testament to the enduring spirit of Ballyknock, a living thread connecting the present to the distant past. She wanted to honour that. But the stranger… he saw them as a weapon. Or a commodity. And when he realized Gladys was getting closer to the heart of it, closer to the families he felt were keeping him in the dark, his approach became more… insistent. More threatening."

"Did she mention feeling threatened by him?" O'Connell pressed. "Did she say he acted aggressively towards her?"

"She said he was persistent," Maeve replied softly. "That he kept showing up, asking more questions, trying to draw her into his own narrative. She mentioned she was becoming uncomfortable, but she still felt a sense of obligation, a historian's duty, to hear him out, to understand his perspective, even if she disagreed with it. She was so focused on the historical significance, on the purity of the academic pursuit, that I don't think she fully grasped the real-world implications, the very human stakes involved."

Maeve picked up one of Gladys's transcribed notes, her fingers trembling slightly as she held it. "This is her translation of some of the symbols found on the standing stones at Cailleach's Embrace. She believed they were instructions, a form of mnemonic to guide participants through a particular ritual. She was so proud of this decipherment. She saw it as a breakthrough, a key to understanding the practical application of these ancient beliefs. But to the families who still adhere to these ways, this level of detail, this… public exposure of their most sacred knowledge, would be unthinkable."

"So, the stranger might have seen this translation as his opportunity?" O'Connell ventured.

"It's highly probable," Maeve agreed. "If he believed Gladys was about to reveal secrets that belonged to his lineage, or that he felt entitled to, he might have acted to stop her, or to claim the knowledge for himself. And given his contentious relationship with the established keepers of these traditions, he might have sought to use Gladys's findings to either discredit them, or to force their hand."

O'Connell remained silent, absorbing her words. The picture that was emerging was one of a complex, deeply rooted community tradition, one that was fiercely guarded, and a desperate, resentful descendant of those guardians who saw an outsider's research as a means to his own ends. And Gladys, caught in the middle, a historian with a relentless drive for truth, had become a target.

"Finn told me Gladys was asking about the 'ingredients' of the rituals," O'Connell said, his gaze sharp. "He said she was learning the specifics. What were these ingredients, Maeve? What did Gladys discover that was so sensitive?"

Maeve closed her eyes for a brief moment, as if bracing herself. "The offerings," she said, her voice barely a whisper, "were not merely symbolic. They were tied to the cycles of nature, to specific times of the year, and to particular… elements. In the earliest iterations, and in some of the more esoteric, still-practiced forms, they involved… natural components that were believed to hold potent energies. Some were benign – rare herbs, specific types of sea salt, carefully harvested seaweed. Others…" She trailed off, her lips pressed into a thin line.

"Others?" O'Connell urged, his patience wearing thin.

"Others involved things that are… less palatable to modern sensibilities," Maeve admitted reluctantly. "The legend of the sacrificed priestess, while sensationalized, hinted at a deeper truth. The sacrifices were not always inanimate. They were intended to be valuable, to represent the greatest offerings that could be given. And for a community so dependent on the sea, that meant life. Not necessarily human life, not in recent history, but… animal life. Sacrifices made at specific points in the lunar cycle, or during periods of great environmental upheaval, to ensure the sea's favour."

O'Connell felt a cold knot form in his stomach. "Animal sacrifices? What kind of animals?"

"Those that were plentiful, yet still represented a significant loss," Maeve said, her voice strained. "The catches that were deemed 'unworthy' for human consumption, or the young of certain species. It was a deeply ingrained belief that to receive the sea's bounty, one had to give a portion of it back, a portion of equal or greater value. And these rituals, while ostensibly fading, were still maintained by a select few families, kept alive in secret, passed down through generations, often shrouded in symbolic language to distance themselves from the harsher realities of their origins."

"And this stranger," O'Connell said, his mind racing, "was he privy to this knowledge? Did he know about these specific practices?"

"I suspect he knew enough to be dangerous," Maeve replied. "He likely came from a family that held some of this knowledge, but perhaps felt excluded from the current custodianship, or disagreed with their interpretation. He saw Gladys as someone who could validate his claims, or amplify his grievances. He was a man who felt entitled, Detective, and he saw these ancient traditions as his birthright, a power he felt was being denied to him."

Maeve looked down at the fragments of pottery again, her fingers brushing against a shard with a faint, etched symbol. "Gladys was trying to document everything, to understand the evolution of these practices. She was meticulous. She was correlating the historical accounts with the physical evidence, like these shards, and her own interviews with people like Finn. She was building a comprehensive picture of a tradition that many in Ballyknock preferred to keep buried deep. And the stranger, I fear, saw her as either an ally to be manipulated, or an obstacle to be removed."

She finally looked up, her gaze meeting O'Connell's with a new urgency. "I tried to tell her to be cautious, that her historical pursuit was leading her into a place where the past was not just studied, but lived, and fiercely protected. I saw her growing fascination, her immersion in the very heart of it, and I recognised the potential for danger. When she started speaking about the stranger's increasingly aggressive attempts to gain her confidence, to extract information, that's when my concern turned to genuine fear. I realized she was no longer just a historian uncovering the past; she was a potential threat to a carefully guarded present."

Maeve's voice softened, laced with a profound regret. "She was so passionate, Detective. So dedicated to her work. She believed that understanding these traditions, in their entirety, was essential to understanding Ballyknock itself. But some truths, however historically significant, can carry a weight that is too heavy for even the most dedicated scholar to bear alone. And I fear that the weight of Ballyknock's hidden past, and the desperate actions of those who sought to control it, ultimately proved too much for her." The silence that followed was thick with unspoken fears, the weight of Maeve's confession settling heavily in the quiet study, painting a stark and dangerous picture of the unseen forces at play in the small, coastal village.

The Threat to the Community

The revelation from Maeve painted a far more complex and unsettling picture than O'Connell had initially imagined. It wasn't just about a historical curiosity Gladys had stumbled upon; it was about the very foundations of Ballyknock's identity, a deeply ingrained system of beliefs and practices that had been meticulously guarded for centuries. The elders, those stoic figures he'd encountered in hushed conversations at the pub or seen tending their fishing nets with weathered hands, were not merely custodians of lore; they were the living embodiments of these traditions, their lives interwoven with the ebb and flow of the sea and the rituals that sought to appease it. Gladys's meticulous research, her insatiable desire to document and understand, was perceived by them not as academic pursuit, but as a profound and dangerous transgression.

O'Connell could now see the fear in the eyes of certain villagers, the way some would turn away when he approached, their faces a mask of polite but firm resistance. It wasn't simply a fear of an outsider asking questions; it was a primal, deeply rooted apprehension that her probing could unravel the delicate tapestry of their existence. These were people who lived by the sea, whose livelihoods, whose very survival, depended on its capricious moods. For generations, they had appeased it, coaxed it, and pleaded with it through methods that, while alien to modern understanding, were vital to their worldview. Gladys, with her modern tools of archaeology and textual analysis, was threatening to expose the "how" and "why" behind these appeasements, potentially demystifying practices that held immense power precisely because of their veiled nature.

The whispers O'Connell had overheard in the village were no longer just idle gossip. They were the murmurings of a community in genuine distress, a collective anxiety about what Gladys might unearth and what that unearthing might mean for them. He remembered Finn's grim pronouncements, how the fisherman had spoken of how quickly Gladys was learning the 'language' of these old ways, how some people wouldn't like it. It wasn't just the stranger who posed a threat; it was the collective body of those who considered themselves the true keepers of Ballyknock's heritage, those who saw Gladys's quest for knowledge as a betrayal, a potential exposé that could shatter their carefully maintained façade.

He thought back to his initial interviews, to the polite stonewalling from the harbourmaster, the evasiveness of the older women at the market. They had spoken of tradition with a reverence that bordered on dogma. They'd emphasized the importance of respecting the past, of not disturbing what was meant to remain undisturbed. At the time, O'Connell had dismissed it as small-town reticence, the natural inclination of a close-knit community to protect its secrets from outsiders. Now, he understood it was something far more potent: a fierce, protective instinct, honed by generations of reliance on the very traditions Gladys was dissecting. They saw her as a foreign element, a catalyst for disruption, a potential harbinger of change that could irrevocably alter their way of life, perhaps even sever their connection to the very sea that sustained them.

The threat wasn't confined to a single individual, nor solely to the estranged descendant Maeve had described. It was a community-wide undercurrent, a collective apprehension that had a tangible, potentially dangerous, manifestation. The elders, in their quiet authority, could wield significant influence. If they perceived Gladys as a genuine threat to the continuity of their practices, their methods of protection might be far more insidious and far-reaching than O'Connell had anticipated. They might not resort to overt violence, but to a subtler, more pervasive form of coercion — ostracization, manipulation, or even the orchestration of 'accidents' that would serve to discourage further investigation.

He recalled the incident at the ruins, the way the area had been cordoned off with an unofficial, yet universally respected, air of finality by some of the older villagers. It had felt less like preservation of an archaeological site and more like the guarding of a sacred, inviolable space. Gladys, by her very nature, had breached that sanctity. Her desire to excavate, to categorize, to understand the context of the artifacts, was seen by these guardians as a defilement. They valued the tangible remnants not for their historical significance, but for their ritualistic weight, for the continued power they held within the existing traditions. To them, Gladys was not uncovering history; she was disturbing the spiritual equilibrium of their community.

The fear Gladys had evoked was not born of malice, necessarily, but of a deep-seated conviction that her actions endangered something sacred. It was the fear of the unknown consequences that could arise from revealing secrets that had, by design, remained hidden. They feared that by bringing these practices into the light of modern scrutiny, they would lose their efficacy, their potency, and their ability to protect the community from the sea's wrath. This made multiple individuals, not just the stranger, potential suspects. Anyone who felt their way of life was threatened by Gladys's research, anyone who adhered rigidly to the old ways, could have felt compelled to act. The list of potential perpetrators was not a short one, but rather a broad spectrum of the community, united by a shared, potent fear.

O'Connell's mind drifted back to the 'offerings' Maeve had described, the natural components that were believed to hold potent energies. He thought of the fragmented pottery, the weathered stones, the woven effigies – all seemingly innocuous remnants of the past. But he now understood they were more than mere artifacts. They were the tools of a deeply ingrained system, the physical manifestations of beliefs that dictated the rhythm of life in Ballyknock. Gladys's quest to understand these tools, to catalogue their use and significance, was what had put her in peril. She was, in essence, unearthing the village's deepest, most vulnerable secrets, and the community, in its collective, ancient wisdom, was prepared to defend those secrets with a ferocity that belied its quiet exterior. The threat was indeed unseen, woven into the very fabric of the village, a silent guardian of traditions that, when threatened, could become a formidable adversary.

CHAPTER FIVE — THE HEART OF THE STORM

The Unidentified Strangers Motive

O'Connell found himself adrift in a sea of conjecture, the chilling realization settling over him like a shroud. The threat wasn't an abstract concept, nor was it confined to the monolithic entity of the village elders and their ancient customs. It had a face, a name, albeit an unknown one, and a history deeply intertwined with the very community he was investigating. His thoughts, previously scattered across the collective apprehension of Ballyknock, now honed in on a singular, unsettling possibility: the unidentified stranger. Maeve's hushed revelation about a banished former resident, someone who had dared to commodify their sacred heritage, had planted a seed of a new, far more tangible hypothesis. This wasn't just about protecting tradition from external scrutiny; it was about the bitter resentment of an outcast, a score to settle with the village that had cast them out.

He worked the phones, his voice resonating with a newfound urgency that surprised even himself. Interpol's resources, usually occupied with far graver international crimes, proved surprisingly accommodating when O'Connell framed his request in terms of potential endangerment and cross-border complicity. He cross-referenced visitor logs from the small mainland ferry service, the only viable route for anyone coming to or leaving Ballyknock with any regularity. The entries were sparse, often cryptic, but a pattern began to emerge, a ghost in the machine of Ballyknock's isolated existence. A name, or rather a series of aliases, flickered on the screen: individuals who had come and gone with unusual frequency over the past few years, often leaving no trace beyond a fleeting transaction. It was a painstaking process, sifting through superficial data, searching for the faintest echo of someone who belonged, yet didn't belong.

Then, a breakthrough. A more detailed visitor log, painstakingly maintained by a retired postal worker who had a penchant for local history and a distrust of modern data entry, provided a crucial piece of the puzzle. It detailed a former resident, someone who had lived in Ballyknock in their youth, a name that had been whispered in hushed tones by Maeve during their earlier conversation. This individual, ostracized years ago, had indeed attempted to leverage Ballyknock's unique heritage for personal gain. There had been talk of a crude attempt to market artisanal crafts based on ancient symbols, a venture that had been met with swift and severe disapproval by the community's gatekeepers. The details were fuzzy, the shame of the transgression too potent for most to openly discuss, but the narrative was clear: this person had been cast out, their connection to the village severed, their name a byword for betrayal.

O'Connell felt a cold dread coil in his gut. This wasn't the primal, instinctual fear of the elders protecting their way of life. This was something far more calculated, far more personal. This ostracized individual, whoever they were, had a vested interest in the secrets of Ballyknock, a desire not just to preserve them, but to exploit them. Gladys, with her academic rigor and her seemingly innocent pursuit of knowledge, had become a pawn, or perhaps an unwitting accomplice, in this stranger's machitate plans. The stranger hadn't approached Gladys out of genuine interest in her research, but as an opportunity. An opportunity to gain access to the very secrets they had been exiled for attempting to profit from. Perhaps they intended to manipulate Gladys, to glean the most valuable information from her findings, or even to coerce her into revealing the full extent of her discoveries.

Alternatively, and more chillingly, the stranger might have viewed Gladys not as a tool, but as a rival. If Gladys was on the verge of uncovering something truly significant, something that could be monetized or wielded as a weapon, then silencing her would be the most direct route to achieving their own objectives. The stranger's motive, therefore, was a potent brew of greed and a deep-seated desire for revenge against the community that had rejected them. They saw Ballyknock's heritage as a commodity, and Gladys's research as the key to unlocking its market value. Her success would be their triumph, her failure their ultimate vindication.

O'Connell leaned back in his chair, the rough texture of the ferry's waiting room upholstery a stark contrast to the polished surfaces of his usual informants. The sheer audacity of it was almost breathtaking. To be cast out and then to return, not to seek reconciliation, but to exploit the very thing that led to their banishment, using an unsuspecting researcher as their unwitting proxy. It reeked of a calculated long game, a festering resentment that had finally found its outlet. He imagined the stranger observing Gladys from a distance, a shadow lurking at the edges of her investigations, carefully gauging her progress, waiting for the opportune moment to intervene.

The nature of this intervention was what troubled O'Connell most. Was it a subtle manipulation, a whispered suggestion that steered her research in a particular direction, or perhaps a more direct confrontation, a desperate attempt to steal her findings? Or had it escalated to something far more sinister? The possibility that Gladys had been silenced, not by the collective will of the village, but by the singular ambition of this disgraced former resident, sent a fresh wave of unease through him. This was no longer about protecting ancient ways from modernization; it was about personal vendetta and avarice cloaked in the guise of historical curiosity.

He pulled out his notebook, the pen scratching against the page as he began to sketch out a profile of this potential antagonist. They would be resourceful, cunning, and deeply embittered. Years of exile would have honed their observational skills, their ability to read people and situations, and their capacity for ruthless action. They would understand the value of Ballyknock's secrets, not just in monetary terms, but in terms of power and influence. They would have the intimate knowledge of the village's rhythms, its blind spots, and its vulnerabilities, making them a far more dangerous adversary than any outsider could ever be. They would know *who* to target, *when* to strike, and *how* to do it with minimal external notice.

The stranger's familiarity with Ballyknock's customs, their understanding of the deep-seated beliefs and rituals, would be a double-edged sword. It would allow them to blend in, to observe without raising suspicion, and to anticipate the reactions of the villagers. It would also, paradoxically, be the very thing they sought to exploit. They would know which secrets were most valuable, which traditions held the most power, and how to twist them to their own advantage. This knowledge, once the source of their shame, would now be their weapon.

O'Connell considered the timeline. Gladys's disappearance had followed a period of intense research, a time when she had likely unearthed information that was particularly sensitive, either to the village elders or to this particular former resident. Had the stranger been monitoring her progress, waiting for her to stumble upon a specific artifact or piece of lore that held the key to their own agenda? Had Gladys, in her unbridled enthusiasm, confided in the wrong person, inadvertently revealing the true depth of her discoveries to someone who saw only opportunity?

The motive was clear: profit and vindication. But the method remained a terrifying enigma. The stranger might have been the one to lure Gladys away from the village, perhaps under the pretense of offering assistance or revealing a hidden aspect of her research. Or perhaps they had simply waited for her to venture out alone, to explore a more remote location where they could act with impunity. The lack of witnesses, the isolated nature of Ballyknock's surroundings, all pointed to a deliberate and carefully planned act.

He had to assume the worst. Gladys wasn't just missing; she was a victim of a calculated crime, orchestrated by someone who understood the currency of Ballyknock's secrets and was willing to go to extreme lengths to control them. The question now was not just *why* but *how*. How had this stranger managed to achieve their objective without immediate detection? What was the nature of their interaction with Gladys?

O'Connell's mind raced, piecing together fragments of conversations, the subtle shifts in villagers' demeanors, the hushed whispers that now seemed to carry a far more sinister weight. The stranger wasn't just a disgruntled former resident; they were a predator who had identified their prey and had expertly exploited the existing vulnerabilities within the community. Their knowledge of the village, their past experiences of ostracism, had made them uniquely equipped to operate in the shadows, to orchestrate events without leaving a clear trail.

He pictured the stranger, perhaps watching Gladys from a hidden vantage point, observing her fascination with the ancient stones, her meticulous documentation of the village's maritime lore. They would have seen her as a means to an end, a conduit to the wealth of knowledge that had been denied to them. Their revenge wouldn't be overt; it would be insidious, a slow-burning resentment that had finally ignited, manifesting in a desperate act of self-preservation disguised as an opportunity for gain.

The terror lay in the stranger's potential intimacy with Ballyknock's hidden currents. They understood the ebb and flow of local loyalties, the unspoken rules that governed the community. They could have exploited these very systems to their advantage, perhaps by enlisting the unwitting help of someone within the village, or by exploiting the inherent suspicion that already existed towards outsiders. The stranger's motive wasn't merely financial; it was a desperate attempt to reclaim what they believed was rightfully theirs, a twisted form of reclaiming their lost status within the community by controlling its most guarded secrets. Gladys had become the key to unlocking that control, and when she proved to be either unwilling or too adept at securing those secrets for herself, the stranger's carefully constructed plan would have taken a darker turn. The very heritage they sought to exploit had, in a sense, come back to haunt them, forcing their hand in a way that now threatened to engulf them in the same storm they had sought to navigate for personal gain.

The Fisherman's Testimony Under Duress

The salt spray, usually a bracing kiss on Finn's weathered face, now felt like a cold, accusatory mist. He huddled deeper into his oilskins, the rough wool scratching against his neck, a physical manifestation of the unease that had taken root and was now blooming into full-blown panic. O'Connell's steady gaze, a familiar anchor in the swirling chaos of Ballyknock, felt sharper tonight, more probing than ever. The questions, previously gentle probes into the village's quiet rhythms, had begun to zero in, their trajectory unnervingly precise, tracing a path that led directly to Finn himself. He could feel the invisible threads of suspicion tightening around him, each unanswered question a knot in the growing snare.

"You said you last saw Gladys heading towards the old lighthouse road, Finn," O'Connell's voice was low, carrying across the wind-whipped deck of the small fishing boat. "That was before the storm blew in, correct? The one that washed out the tracks to the western cliff?"

Finn's throat felt tight, as if the very air he was trying to draw in was thick with the unsaid. He nodded, his eyes darting towards the churning grey expanse of the sea, as if searching for an answer there, an alibi written in the waves. "Aye, Inspector. She was… she was going that way. Said she had some more research to do, something about the tidal patterns, the way they affected the older settlements." His voice, usually as steady as the dependable rhythm of his fishing, quavered slightly. He'd rehearsed this lie, polished it like the barnacles on his hull, but it felt brittle, fragile against the weight of O'Connell's persistent inquiry.

"And you didn't accompany her?" O'Connell pressed, the question hanging in the air, heavy with unspoken doubt. "You were down by the cove yourself, weren't you? Checking your nets?"

Finn's gaze snapped back to O'Connell. The accusation, veiled but palpable, sent a shiver down his spine. He'd deliberately omitted details, small omissions that now felt like gaping holes in his narrative. He'd wanted to distance himself, to avoid any suggestion of complicity, but in doing so, he'd only painted himself as evasive. "The nets, aye. Just a quick check before the weather turned truly foul. I saw her in the distance, heading towards the lighthouse path. That's all, Inspector. The wind picked up something fierce then, and I had to make sure my boat was secure."

O'Connell remained silent for a long moment, his eyes, the colour of a storm-tossed sea, fixed on Finn's face. It was a look that could strip away layers of carefully constructed composure, a look that seemed to see not just the fisherman, but the man beneath. Finn shifted uncomfortably, the damp chill seeping through his worn woollens. He felt a bead of sweat trickle down his temple, despite the biting wind.

"A quick check," O'Connell repeated, the words a soft exhalation. "Yet the squall that followed was sudden, wasn't it? Came up out of nowhere, they say." He paused, letting the implication hang. "Hardly the sort of weather to be leisurely checking nets, Finn. More the sort of weather to be seeking shelter, or perhaps, if one was already in the vicinity of the cove, to be… observing."

Finn swallowed hard. The truth, a tangled knot of fear and misplaced loyalty, was beginning to unravel within him. He'd seen more than he'd let on. He'd witnessed a clandestine meeting, a shadowed encounter that had gnawed at him ever since. He'd convinced himself it was none of his business, that Gladys, with her modern ways and her insatiable curiosity, was bound to attract attention, perhaps even trouble. But O'Connell's relentless pursuit was forcing his hand, peeling back the layers of his carefully constructed ignorance.

"There was someone else there, wasn't there, Finn?" O'Connell's voice softened, a subtle shift in tone that was more disarming than any accusation. "Near the cove. Someone Gladys met."

The wind howled around them, a mournful lament that seemed to echo Finn's inner turmoil. He looked at the rough, salt-crusted planks of the jetty, at the bobbing fishing boats, at the familiar, yet now alien, landscape of Ballyknock. His silence was a heavy thing, a confession in itself. He thought of Gladys's bright, eager eyes, her earnest belief in the island's mystique, her descent into something darker, something orchestrated.

"Aye," Finn finally admitted, his voice barely a whisper against the rising gale. "Aye, Inspector. There was. I… I didn't say anything because I didn't want to get involved. Didn't want to cause trouble." He hesitated, the words tumbling out now, a dam of suppressed information finally breaking. "It was him. The stranger. The one… the one who'd been asking about the old ways, the one Maeve warned me about."

O'Connell's expression didn't change, but Finn could feel a subtle shift, a tightening of focus. The pieces were clicking into place, the phantom of his suspicion now coalescing into a tangible form. "And what were they doing, Finn? When you saw them?"

Finn's hands clenched into fists. He remembered the scene with sickening clarity. The stranger, cloaked and indistinct in the fading light, standing at the water's edge. Gladys, her silhouette sharp against the darkening sky, approaching him hesitantly. Their hushed conversation, lost to the wind, but the intent palpable. He'd seen the stranger press something into Gladys's hand, something small and dark, glinting faintly as she took it. He'd also seen Gladys's initial hesitation, her reluctance, before she'd finally nodded, her shoulders slumping as if in resignation.

"He met her," Finn said, his voice hoarse. "Down by the cove. Not at the lighthouse road, but closer to the water. He... he'd promised her something, Inspector. Something about the island's secrets. Said it was a... a ritual. A way to truly understand Ballyknock, to connect with the old powers." He paused, the memory of Gladys's earnestness, her misguided faith, a painful stab. "He called it... the 'Invocation of the Tides'."

O'Connell's gaze was unwavering. "And you saw this ritual?"

Finn shook his head, the motion jerky, agitated. "No. Not the ritual itself. I saw them together. He... he was speaking to her, quite intently. And then... he just left her. Turned and walked away, disappearing into the mist rolling in from the sea. Gladys was left standing there, alone, by the water. That's when the storm hit, a proper gale, it was. I... I went to check on my boat. I thought she'd gone back to her cottage. I swear, Inspector, I didn't think she'd be in any real danger. Not like this."

The confession hung in the air, thick with Finn's own guilt and the undeniable truth of Gladys's predicament. His previous account, so carefully constructed to portray him as a mere observer, a man simply going about his business, now felt like a desperate attempt to distance himself from the grim reality of what had transpired. By omitting the stranger's presence, by claiming to have last seen Gladys heading in a different direction, he had, in essence, deliberately obscured the most crucial moments leading up to her disappearance. He hadn't just failed to report; he had actively, if perhaps out of fear, concealed vital information. The full weight of his omission, the terrifying implications of Gladys being left alone with the stranger moments before the tempest, now pressed down on him. He had seen a warning, a clear sign of impending danger, and he had turned away. The 'Invocation of the Tides' – the words themselves sent a tremor through him. It was more than just a ritual; it was a lure, a calculated act of manipulation designed to draw Gladys into a dangerous embrace, an embrace from which she had seemingly not returned. His reticence had, in all likelihood, cost Gladys dearly. The storm that had provided him with cover for his evasiveness, had also, he now realized with sickening certainty, provided the stranger with the perfect cloak for his true intentions, and the perfect environment to ensure Gladys's actions, and her ultimate fate, remained shrouded in the very same tempestuous mystery that now engulfed Ballyknock.

A Desperate Pact

The wind still shrieked its mournful tune around the small fishing boat, a symphony of nature's fury that mirrored the turmoil churning within Finn. He watched O'Connell, the inspector's weathered face set in grim contemplation, as the man carefully sifted through the contents of a small, water-damaged satchel pulled from the debris near the cove. It was a collection of Gladys's belongings, a macabre testament to her final hours. Amidst the soggy notebooks and sodden scraps of paper, O'Connell's fingers, surprisingly gentle for their size, unearthed a small, oilskin-wrapped parcel. The contents were revealed to be a series of letters, their ink blurred but still legible in places, penned in Gladys's distinctive, elegant script.

"She kept meticulous records, our Gladys," O'Connell murmured, his voice barely audible above the tempest's roar. He held up one of the letters, its edges frayed by the salt and spray. "Correspondence with our stranger. It seems your instincts were correct, Finn. She wasn't just meeting him; she was… collaborating."

Finn's stomach twisted. Collaborating. The word felt like another layer of betrayal, another nail in the coffin of his naive belief that Gladys's fascination was merely academic. He had seen the stranger's influence, the subtle shift in her demeanor in the weeks leading up to her disappearance, a growing intensity in her gaze, a withdrawal from her usual vibrant engagement with the village. But he hadn't grasped the extent of it.

O'Connell continued to read, his brow furrowed. "It appears," he began, his voice gaining a sharper edge, "that this 'stranger' presented Gladys with a rather… unconventional proposition. Something about unlocking the island's inherent spiritual energies. A 'cleansing ritual' at the cove, he called it." He looked up at Finn, his eyes piercing. "Gladys, it seems, was quite taken with the idea. She saw it as a way to 'commune with the ancient heart of Ballyknock,' as she puts it here."

The words 'ancient heart' resonated with a chilling familiarity. It was the language of folklore, of the very myths and legends that had drawn Gladys to Ballyknock in the first place. Finn recalled Gladys's impassioned pronouncements, her fervent belief in the island's hidden power, her desire to experience something beyond the mundane. He had dismissed it as youthful enthusiasm, a romantic notion. Now, he realized it was a dangerous vulnerability.

"She believed it was a harmless tradition," O'Connell continued, his voice a low rumble of disbelief. "An old Celtic practice, passed down through generations. She writes about feeling a profound connection to the earth, a shedding of worldly burdens. It's all here, in her own words." He tapped the letter with a calloused finger. "She was eager, even excited, to participate."

Finn's mind raced, piecing together the fragments. The stranger's subtle manipulation, Gladys's yearning for spiritual enlightenment, her willingness to embrace ancient rituals – it was a perfect storm of circumstance. The stranger hadn't simply encountered a curious scholar; he had found a willing, albeit misguided, acolyte.

"But this 'cleansing ritual'," O'Connell said, his tone hardening, "was merely a facade. A carefully crafted deception to mask his true intentions." He held up another letter, this one thicker, more detailed. "He was using her fascination, Finn. Her belief. He saw her as a means to an end, a way to tap into the cove's alleged spiritual energy for his own gain. He's not interested in tradition; he's interested in power, in exploiting this place."

The implication hung heavy in the salty air. The stranger wasn't a fellow enthusiast of local lore; he was a charlatan, a predator who preyed on the naive and the earnest. He had seen Gladys's open heart, her inquisitive mind, and had twisted it to his own nefarious purpose. He had seen her not as a person, but as a tool, a disposable pawn in his game.

"And the cove itself," O'Connell mused, his gaze drifting towards the turbulent horizon, "has always been spoken of in hushed tones. Whispers of its unique properties, its connection to the tides, the moon cycles. The stranger, it seems, understood this. He saw an opportunity to leverage those beliefs, to amplify them, and Gladys was his chosen instrument."

Finn could almost see the scene unfold in his mind's eye: the stranger, with his silken words and his practiced charm, weaving a web of illusion around Gladys. He had likely painted a picture of ancient rites, of a sacred communion, all the while knowing the true purpose was far more selfish, far more sinister. Gladys, blinded by her quest for understanding, had walked willingly into the trap.

"He even hints," O'Connell said, his voice barely a whisper now, as if afraid of disturbing some unseen presence, "that if things went awry, if the 'ritual' drew unwanted attention, she would be the one to bear the brunt of it. He's practically setting her up to take the fall." The words sent a fresh wave of cold dread through Finn. Gladys, the bright, vibrant woman who had filled his quiet village with her infectious energy, had been systematically ensnared, her trust exploited, her very essence manipulated. And he, Finn, had witnessed the early stages of this sinister design and had, through his silence, inadvertently allowed it to unfold. The weight of his inaction, of his fear of entanglement, now felt like an insurmountable burden. He had seen the darkness gathering, and instead of raising a light, he had turned his back. The pact, a desperate agreement born of Gladys's yearning and the stranger's ambition, had been sealed not with ink and paper, but with deception and a chilling disregard for human life. He looked at O'Connell, a silent plea in his eyes, a desperate hope that the inspector's steady hand could somehow untangle the web of lies and bring Gladys back from whatever abyss she had been cast into. The storm raged on, a fitting backdrop to the dark truth that was slowly, agonizingly, coming to light.

The Ritualistic Clues

The storm, though abating slightly, still clawed at the sides of the boat, its fury now a sullen grumble compared to the earlier tempest. Inspector O'Connell, his face etched with the strain of the night's grim discoveries, returned his attention to the waterlogged satchel. The letters, once carefully preserved by Gladys, were now fragile artifacts, their secrets seeping into the damp air. Finn watched, a knot of dread tightening in his gut, as O'Connell meticulously laid out the remaining contents: a small, leather-bound diary, its pages warped and stained, and a collection of loose sheets filled with Gladys's familiar, elegant script. These were not just notes; they were the breadcrumbs left behind, a trail leading Finn deeper into the heart of Ballyknock's ancient, and now terrifying, mysteries.

O'Connell's brow furrowed as he carefully opened the diary. The ink, where not completely obliterated by seawater, revealed a disturbing blend of academic curiosity and an almost feverish devotion. "The 'Cove of Whispers'," he read aloud, his voice a low, resonant rumble against the wind's sigh. "She's described it as a nexus, Finn. A place where the veil between worlds is thinnest. And the stranger... he fed into that belief, didn't he?"

Finn nodded, the memory of Gladys's fervent discussions about Ballyknock's "inherent energies" flashing through his mind. He remembered her excitement, her certainty that she was on the cusp of a profound discovery, a connection to something elemental and ancient. He had seen it as a romantic fascination, a scholar's pursuit of the arcane. Now, it felt like a deliberate luring, a carefully orchestrated descent into a preordained fate.

"She writes about the tides," O'Connell continued, his finger tracing a line of faded ink. "Not just any tides, mind you. Specific lunar cycles. The spring tides, the equinoxes, the solstices… he seems to have been particularly interested in the times of peak tidal surge. 'The mother's breath,' she calls it here, in reference to the sea. And the stranger, this 'Keeper of Lore' as she's named him in here, apparently told her that these surges were moments of immense power, when the island's 'heartbeat' was most palpable."

Finn leaned closer, trying to decipher the blurred words. The stranger's methods were becoming chillingly clear. He hadn't just been engaging Gladys in conversation; he had been meticulously studying Ballyknock's natural rhythms, its ancient lore, and then twisting them to his own dark purpose. The cove wasn't just a secluded spot; it was a calculated stage, and Gladys, his unwitting – or perhaps, increasingly willing – lead actress.

"He instructed her on specific timings," O'Connell stated, his voice taking on a sharper, more definitive tone. "It wasn't enough to be at the cove; she had to be there during a precise window. Look here." He pointed to a passage in the diary, a series of astrological symbols and tidal charts scrawled alongside Gladys's notes. "This indicates a specific time, during the highest tide of the recent spring equinox. A 'confluence of celestial and terrestrial forces,' she's written. He made her believe that this was the only time the ritual would be truly potent."

The pieces clicked into place with a sickening finality. The stranger hadn't just met Gladys at the cove; he had orchestrated her presence there at a moment of extreme natural danger. He had weaponized the sea itself, using its raw power to mask his true intentions. The cove, a place steeped in local legend, a place where tales of drowning and disappearances were whispered on the wind, had been chosen for its very reputation. The stranger had understood that any misfortune there would be easily attributed to the sea's temper, to the island's inherent capriciousness, rather than to human malice.

"And the ritual itself," O'Connell murmured, his gaze unfocused as he processed the information. "It wasn't just about communing. It involved specific incantations, spoken in Old Irish, apparently. She's transcribed some of them here, along with instructions on what to offer." He held up a separate sheet of paper, its edges softened by the damp. "These are offerings to the 'sea spirits,' to appease them, to draw their favour. Sea salt, woven reeds, and… small, carved stones. He supplied her with most of them, it seems. And the incantations…" O'Connell's voice trailed off, a grim realization dawning on his face. "They were designed to draw power, Finn. Not to appease. To harness."

Finn felt a wave of nausea wash over him. He remembered Gladys, her eyes bright with a mixture of academic curiosity and a spiritual yearning, telling him about the importance of respecting ancient traditions, of honouring the forces of nature. He had dismissed it as academic enthusiasm, a romantic embellishment. But now, he saw it for what it truly was: a carefully constructed narrative designed to manipulate her, to make her a willing participant in her own demise. The stranger had played on her deepest desires, her intellectual curiosity, and her spiritual vulnerability, weaving a tapestry of deception that was as intricate as it was deadly.

"He's using the island's folklore against us, against her," O'Connell stated, his voice hard. "Ballyknock has always been a place of superstition, of stories about the sea claiming its own. The stranger weaponized that. He chose a time when the tides were at their most ferocious, when the sea was at its most unpredictable, and then he armed Gladys with rituals that he knew would put her in harm's way. He wanted it to look like an accident, a tragic consequence of her fascination with the island's ancient lore."

The image solidified in Finn's mind: Gladys, standing at the edge of the churning sea, reciting ancient words, her mind filled with the stranger's promises of spiritual enlightenment, unaware that the very ritual meant to connect her to the island's soul was designed to sever her connection to life itself. The stranger, lurking in the shadows, would have watched, waited for the opportune moment, and then allowed the sea to do his dirty work. He had used Gladys's belief in the sacredness of the place to facilitate her destruction.

"The 'heart of the storm'," O'Connell mused, looking out at the grey, heaving expanse of the sea. "That's what she calls the peak of the tidal surge in her notes. The moment of greatest power. He chose that moment, Finn. He ensured she was there, exposed, vulnerable. He manipulated the natural forces, the ancient beliefs, and her own yearning for something more. It's a horrifyingly clever, and utterly ruthless, plan."

Finn's gaze fell upon a particular passage in the diary. Gladys had written, in a shaky hand, about a growing unease, a flicker of doubt. She described a moment when the stranger's explanations seemed to falter, when his eyes, usually so steady and persuasive, held a glint of something cold and calculating. She had noted a discrepancy between the ancient texts she was studying and the stranger's interpretations, a subtle divergence that had pricked her academic instinct. But she had dismissed it, attributing it to the inherent ambiguities of translating such ancient lore.

"She had doubts," Finn said, his voice barely a whisper. "She sensed something wasn't right. She wrote about a feeling… a chill that had nothing to do with the sea spray."

O'Connell nodded, his own face grim. "She was a sharp woman, Gladys. But he was a master manipulator. He likely saw those doubts, those flickers of intuition, and worked harder to suppress them, to reassert his control. He might have even used the impending storm, the rising tides, as further justification, telling her that such powerful forces demanded unwavering focus, absolute faith."

The detail was chilling. The stranger had not only exploited Gladys's belief in Ballyknock's mystical properties but had also weaponized the very environment. He had chosen a specific time, a dangerous tide, a notorious location, and populated it with rituals that, under the guise of appeasement, were designed to harness the volatile power of the sea, all while making it appear as a natural, tragic occurrence. Gladys, eager to uncover the island's secrets, had become the unwitting catalyst for a meticulously planned demise, orchestrated by a man who saw her not as a fellow explorer of ancient mysteries, but as a disposable pawn in a far more sinister game. The stranger was not merely interested in Ballyknock's lore; he was interested in exploiting its power, and Gladys was his chosen vessel. He had seen her intellect, her passion, her yearning for meaning, and had twisted it all into a weapon against her. The storm was not just a backdrop; it was an accomplice, a force of nature enlisted in a human-engineered tragedy.

"He left her exposed," O'Connell stated, his voice heavy with accusation. "He used her deep respect for these ancient ways, her desire to connect with the island's 'spirit,' to lure her into a situation where the natural elements, amplified by his twisted rituals, would do his bidding. The incantations, the offerings… they weren't acts of reverence, Finn. They were meticulously designed steps, designed to coincide with the peak of the surge, to create a scenario that would look like a tragic accident. A woman lost to the sea during a particularly dangerous tide, following old, obscure rituals. Who would question it?"

The implication was damning. The stranger had used Gladys's own research, her own fascination, as the blueprint for her murder. He had turned her academic pursuits into the very means of her destruction. The sea, a force of nature so often personified in folklore, had been enlisted as an unwitting accomplice, its raw power magnified and directed by a human hand that sought only to control and to conceal. The cove, with its eerie reputation, its connection to the lunar cycles and the ocean's immense power, had been the chosen stage. And Gladys, drawn by the siren song of ancient knowledge, had become the ultimate sacrifice, her very belief system exploited to ensure her demise was attributed to the unforgiving embrace of the sea. The stranger hadn't just orchestrated a ritual; he had orchestrated a meticulously planned murder, cloaked in the guise of ancient tradition and the fury of the elements.

"She writes about the 'heart of the storm'," O'Connell repeated, his gaze fixed on the turbulent grey horizon. "The peak of the tide, when the sea's energy is at its zenith. He chose that precise moment. He made sure she was there, exposed, vulnerable. He used the island's reputation, its folklore, its natural cycles, and Gladys's own earnest desire to connect with it all, to create the perfect cover. It's… it's monstrously intelligent."

Finn felt a cold dread seep into his bones. He remembered Gladys's eager descriptions of the cove, her almost reverent tone when speaking of its unique atmosphere, its connection to the ebb and flow of the tides. He had seen it as a romantic obsession, a scholarly pursuit. Now, he saw it as a carefully constructed trap, baited with the promise of ancient secrets and spiritual enlightenment. The stranger had not just found a willing student; he had found a perfect victim, someone whose deepest desires made her susceptible to his dark machinations. He had seen her curiosity as a weakness to be exploited, her passion as a tool to be wielded.

"He gave her specific instructions," O'Connell continued, his voice low and measured, as if the very act of speaking these words aloud could conjure the ghost of the stranger's plan. "He told her exactly when to be at the cove, what to say, what to offer. He knew that the old tales, the superstitions surrounding the cove, would provide the perfect alibi. If something happened, it would simply be the sea, claiming another soul, as it had done countless times before."

The chilling efficiency of the plan was terrifying. The stranger hadn't just engineered a situation; he had woven a narrative, a tapestry of ancient lore and natural forces, designed to obscure his involvement. He had transformed Gladys's genuine interest in Ballyknock's spiritual heritage into the very mechanism of her destruction. The rituals, the incantations, the offerings – these were not acts of devotion, but carefully calibrated steps in a deadly sequence, timed to coincide with the most dangerous moments of the tidal surge. The cove, a place already shrouded in mystery and whispered warnings, had become the ultimate stage for a meticulously crafted murder, where the elements themselves were intended to serve as both the weapon and the witness, ensuring that the truth remained buried beneath the relentless churn of the ocean. The stranger had played on the island's deep-seated reputation for swallowing people whole, making Gladys's fate appear as just another tragic chapter in Ballyknock's storied, and fearsome, history.

"He even coached her on how to present it," O'Connell added, his eyes scanning the cryptic notes. "To make it seem like a natural progression of her research, a culmination of her studies into the island's unique spiritual energies. She was to appear unafraid, even eager, to embrace these ancient practices. He wanted her to be seen as a willing participant, not a victim. And then, when the tide turned, when the sea's fury was at its peak, he would simply let nature take its course, ensuring that her disappearance would be attributed to the cove's notorious dangers."

Finn's mind reeled. He saw Gladys, her face illuminated by the moonlight on a previous visit to the cove, her voice filled with an almost evangelical fervor as she spoke of the island's ancient heart. He had listened, perhaps too passively, too unwilling to confront the intensity of her beliefs. Now, he realized that her intensity had been precisely what the stranger had sought, a beacon that drew her into his carefully constructed web. He had seen her passion not as a sign of a vibrant spirit, but as an opportunity to be exploited, a weakness to be leveraged. The stranger had used the very essence of Ballyknock, its raw, untamed power, its ancient lore, and Gladys's fervent belief in it all, to engineer a murder that would be as seamless as the tide itself. The storm, which had once seemed merely a backdrop to their conversation, now felt like a malevolent force, an accomplice to the stranger's wicked design, amplifying the tragic tableau he had so meticulously crafted. The sea, in its immense, indifferent power, was to be his accomplice, his scapegoat.

Confrontation at the Cove

The air still tasted of salt and the recent tempest, a briny kiss that clung to O'Connell's coat and Finn's hair. The sky, a bruised expanse of grey and bruised purple, offered little respite. The sea, however, had begun its insistent push inland, the rising tide licking at the weathered rocks of Cailleach's Embrace with renewed vigor. It was a primal rhythm, the pulse of Ballyknock's untamed heart, and O'Connell, his jaw set, his eyes narrowed against the spray, was walking directly into its embrace. Finn followed, a shadow at his heels, the weight of Gladys's fate pressing down on him with every crashing wave. The cove, which had held such a potent, almost mystical allure for Gladys, now felt like a gaping maw, ready to swallow them whole. The legend of the 'Cove of Whispers' was no longer a quaint piece of folklore; it was a chilling testament to the stranger's calculated cruelty.

O'Connell moved with a practiced urgency, his gaze sweeping the treacherous terrain. The crevice Gladys had mentioned in her final, desperate notes, the one where she believed the stranger had hidden his true intentions, was their destination. The churning water made the footing precarious, each step a gamble against the slippery, seaweed-slicked stones. The stranger, as O'Connell had predicted, was there. A solitary figure, silhouetted against the churning sea, his movements furtive and quick as he scrabbled at a dark recess in the rock face, just above the surging waterline. The same kind of recess where one might hide something, or perhaps, retrieve something.

"Hold it right there!" O'Connell's voice, usually a calm, authoritative rumble, was now a bark, sharp and commanding, cutting through the roar of the surf.

The figure startled, spinning around with a panicked speed that betrayed his guilt. It was him. The stranger, or whoever he truly was. His face, usually a mask of serene contemplation, was contorted with a mixture of surprise and something akin to primal fear. He had the same unnervingly clear eyes, the same lean, almost ascetic build, but in the harsh light of the cove, and the weight of O'Connell's accusation, a darkness seemed to cling to him, like the sea mist that coiled around the jagged rocks.

"What do you want?" the stranger demanded, his voice higher than Finn remembered, laced with a tremor that had nothing to do with the cold. He clutched something to his chest, a dark, nondescript object that was partially obscured by his oilskin jacket.

"We want the truth," O'Connell stated, his gaze locked on the object in the stranger's hands. "And we want to know what you did to Gladys."

The stranger's eyes darted from O'Connell to Finn, then back to the unforgiving sea. He took a step back, his boots slipping on the wet stone. "She… she was lost in the storm," he stammered, his voice barely audible above the din. "The tides… they were stronger than I anticipated."

"Stronger than you anticipated?" O'Connell's voice dripped with incredulity. "You knew the tides. You studied them. You used them, didn't you? You used Gladys's fascination with them, her belief in their power, to your own ends."

The stranger flinched, his grip tightening on the object he held. "I… I advised her. I shared lore. I never intended for her to be harmed."

"Advised her?" Finn's voice was rough, choked with a grief that had been simmering for too long. He pushed past O'Connell, stepping onto the slippery rocks, closer to the man who had stolen Gladys from him. "You told her when to be here. You told her what to do. You orchestrated this entire charade, didn't you? You made her believe that this place, this ritual, was the key to some ancient truth. But it was all a lie, wasn't it? A way to get rid of her."

The stranger's eyes widened, a flicker of something unreadable – perhaps regret, perhaps fear – passing through them. "It wasn't supposed to be like this," he began, his voice barely a whisper. "My plan... it was to use the island's energies, to draw upon its deep well of power. Gladys... she was a conduit. A willing participant in a ritual that was meant to unlock something profound."

"Unlock what?" O'Connell pressed, his tone relentless. "And what was Gladys's role in this grand unlocking? Was she the sacrifice?"

A wave crashed higher than the rest, sending a spray of icy water over them. The stranger stumbled back, losing his footing for a perilous moment before regaining his balance. The object he was clutching slipped from his grasp, clattering onto the rocks. It was a small, intricately carved wooden bird, its wings spread as if in flight. Finn recognized it instantly; Gladys had shown him one just like it, a gift she said the stranger had given her, a symbol of freedom and spiritual ascent. Now, it seemed like a mockery.

"She was meant to be... attuned," the stranger said, his voice strained. He made a desperate lunge for the wooden bird, but O'Connell was quicker, intercepting him with a firm hand on his arm.

"Attuned to what, exactly?" O'Connell's grip tightened. "To the bottom of the sea? To the cold embrace of oblivion?"

The stranger's eyes, so calm and assured in their previous encounters, were now wild, desperate. "The rituals... they were designed to channel the storm's fury. To harness the raw power of the sea at its peak. I believed that by aligning with the lunar cycles, the tidal surges, we could achieve a state of... amplified consciousness. Gladys was integral to that. Her understanding of the lore, her sensitivity... she was the perfect anchor."

"Anchor?" Finn echoed, his voice raw with disbelief. "She was your bait, wasn't she? Your willing pawn, sent to the most dangerous place at the most dangerous time, armed with your lies."

"No!" the stranger exclaimed, his voice rising in a desperate pitch. "I never wanted her dead. I... I confess, I saw an opportunity. The island's history, its folklore, the very nature of this cove... it all spoke of a power that could be tapped. Gladys's research, her passion, made her the ideal partner. I fed her theories, amplified her beliefs. I convinced her that this was a significant moment, a confluence of ancient energies."

He gestured vaguely towards the crevice he had been searching. "I was looking for... for a marker. Something she had placed there, a final symbol of her connection to the ritual. I thought... I thought if I could retrieve it, perhaps I could... make sense of it all."

"Make sense of her death?" O'Connell's voice was cold, unforgiving. "You left her, didn't you? When the storm hit its peak, when the waves began to pull her under, you ran. You abandoned her to the very forces you claimed to control."

The stranger's gaze fell to the ground, his shoulders slumping. The bravado had evaporated, replaced by a chilling admission. "The storm… it became uncontrollable. The currents were ferocious. She… she was struggling. I tried to… to reach her. But the waves… they were immense. The undertow…" He paused, his voice catching. "It was too much. I couldn't… I couldn't save her. And to stay… it would have meant facing the same fate. I… I retreated. I couldn't… I couldn't be swallowed by it too."

The confession hung in the air, thick and suffocating. He hadn't just planned her death; he had witnessed it, or at least, he had chosen to survive it, leaving Gladys to the unforgiving embrace of the sea. The meticulous planning, the exploitation of lore, it all served a singular purpose: to provide cover, to ensure that when the inevitable happened, it would be attributed to the capricious nature of the sea, not to the deliberate actions of a man.

"So, you let her drown," Finn stated, the words a stark, brutal accusation. "You watched her struggle, and you chose to save yourself. You used her, you manipulated her, and when your grand ritual went wrong, you left her to die alone."

The stranger looked up, his eyes filled with a desperate plea. "It was an accident. A tragic miscalculation. I never intended for the ritual to go awry like that. The lore… it spoke of harnessing power, not of succumbing to it. I thought I understood the tides, the energies. I was wrong. I was so terribly wrong."

"Wrong?" O'Connell scoffed, the sound harsh and devoid of sympathy. "You were wrong to believe you could play God with ancient forces. You were wrong to exploit Gladys's trust, her intellect, her very soul. And you were wrong to think you could get away with murder." He took a step forward, his face grim. "Where is the evidence, then? The 'marker' you were so desperate to retrieve? The truth that Gladys tried so hard to uncover before you silenced her?"

The stranger gestured weakly towards the crevice. "It's… it's in there. Something she… she entrusted to me. A small amulet. She believed it amplified her connection to the sea spirits. I was… I was going to use it as proof that I had tried to help her, that she had made a sacrifice. But then… I realised it might also implicate me further. It held her essence, her intent. I didn't know what to do with it."

O'Connell pushed past Finn, his movements purposeful. He reached into the crevice, his fingers brushing against something cold and smooth. He pulled out a small, intricately carved object – not the wooden bird, but a polished piece of sea glass, etched with ancient symbols. It was unmistakably Gladys's work, imbued with the same meticulous artistry that characterized all her research.

"This," O'Connell said, holding it up, the sea glass catching the faint light, "this is what she was trying to tell us. The truth you tried to bury. This isn't just a trinket. This is her final message." He turned his gaze back to the stranger, his expression unyielding. "And you, you were trying to retrieve it not to help her, but to destroy the last vestige of her presence, the last piece of evidence that pointed to your culpability."

The stranger remained silent, his gaze fixed on the sea glass, a silent testament to his betrayal. The rising tide continued its relentless assault on the shore, the waves crashing against the rocks with a ferocity that seemed to mirror the turmoil in Finn's own heart. He looked at the stranger, the man who had woven a web of deception around Gladys, who had preyed on her intellect and her passion, and who had ultimately left her to the mercy of the very elements she had sought to understand. The storm might have abated, but the true storm, the one that had ripped Gladys from their lives, had been a man-made tempest, brewed in the dark corners of ambition and fueled by a chilling disregard for human life. Cailleach's Embrace had indeed been the heart of the storm, and its true nature had been laid bare, not by ancient spirits, but by the cruel machinations of a man.

CHAPTER SIX - ECHOES ON THE WIND

The Strangers Confession and Capture

The sea had begun to withdraw its icy fingers from the shore, leaving behind a slick, glistening testament to its recent fury. The wind, though still keen, had lost its tempestuous roar, settling into a mournful sigh that whispered through the skeletal remains of kelp and driftwood scattered across the cove. Dawn, a hesitant blush of rose and lavender, was beginning to paint the eastern sky, its nascent light gradually eroding the suffocating darkness that had enveloped their desperate confrontation. O'Connell's grip on the stranger's arm was like a vise, his knuckles white against the worn fabric of the man's oilskin jacket. The stranger, his face pale and gaunt in the emerging light, offered no resistance. The defiant glint in his eyes had been extinguished, replaced by a defeated slump of his shoulders, a physical manifestation of his confession.

"It was... a confluence of factors," the stranger finally managed, his voice raspy, as if the words themselves were an effort. "The island's power, as described in the ancient texts... it's undeniable. And Gladys... she was so eager, so full of conviction. She believed she was on the cusp of something extraordinary, a true communion with the primal forces of this place." He swallowed hard, his Adam's apple bobbing in his thin throat. "I... I played upon that. I amplified her theories, embellished the lore. I convinced her that the storm, this particular convergence of celestial and terrestrial energies, was the opportune moment. A moment for unparalleled discovery."

O'Connell's expression remained impassive, a granite mask carved by years of facing the harsh realities of life in Ballyknock. "Discovery of what, precisely? And at what cost?"

The stranger's gaze drifted towards the retreating waves, a flicker of something that might have been remorse, or perhaps just a profound, bone-deep weariness, crossing his features. "The texts spoke of artifacts, remnants of forgotten rituals, imbued with potent energies. They were said to be revealed during periods of intense elemental flux, when the veil between worlds thinned. I believed Gladys, with her intuitive understanding of the island's subtle currents, could help me locate them. She was... invaluable. More so than I initially realised."

Finn watched the exchange, a cold knot of anger tightening in his gut. Invaluable. Gladys, reduced to a tool, a means to an end in this man's avaricious quest. "So, you used her," Finn stated, his voice flat, devoid of the emotion that threatened to consume him. "You fed her ambition, her fascination with the island's mysteries, to lure her into a trap.

You knew the storm was coming, didn't you? You planned for her to be here."

The stranger flinched at Finn's direct accusation. "I didn't *plan* for her to… to perish," he insisted, his voice gaining a desperate edge. "I anticipated risk, of course. Such pursuits always carry inherent dangers. But I believed we could manage them. I thought I had accounted for the tides, for the wind's caprice. My focus was on the artifacts, on the knowledge they contained. The lore spoke of a great power, a connection to the very lifeblood of the island, and I craved that understanding. Gladys's passion was… contagious. It drew me in, too. It blinded me to the ultimate peril."

"Blinded you?" O'Connell's voice was a low growl. "Or did it merely serve as a convenient excuse when your avarice outpaced your caution? You saw a chance, didn't you? A chance to seize these so-called artifacts, to profit from their perceived power, and to ensure that no one else, particularly Gladys, could reveal your deception. If she disappeared, along with any evidence of her 'participation,' your narrative would be unchallenged. A tragic accident, a victim of the sea's unforgiving nature."

The stranger looked directly at O'Connell, his eyes wide and pleading, yet holding a desperate, fragile truth. "It was not entirely like that," he stammered. "I… I did intend to retrieve something for her. Something she believed was a key, a personal connection to the island's spirit. She entrusted it to me before the worst of the storm hit. I was to keep it safe, to perhaps use it in a subsequent ritual, one that would have been far more controlled. But the storm… it overwhelmed everything. The waves were… monstrous. They were not merely powerful; they were malevolent."

He trailed off, a shiver wracking his frame, though the wind had lessened its bite. "I was on a higher ledge, trying to secure some of the more delicate instruments I had brought. Gladys was further down, closer to the water's edge, making some final observations. When the rogue wave came... it was unlike anything I had ever witnessed. It didn't just crash; it seemed to engulf the entire cove. I saw her... I saw her swept away. And in that moment, my instinct was survival. To stay would have meant certain death."

"So, you ran," Finn said, the words tasting like ash in his mouth. "You ran and left her to drown."

"I retreated," the stranger corrected, his voice barely a whisper. "I tried to get to her, but the current was too strong. It pulled everything in its path. I saw her disappear beneath the churning water. And then... I realized I was in danger too. The very forces I had sought to harness were turning on me. I had to save myself. I had to live to... to understand what had happened. To perhaps even find a way to honour her memory."

O'Connell stepped closer, his shadow falling over the stranger. "Honour her memory by hiding the truth? By letting the island's untamed spirit bear the blame for your calculated actions? You speak of artifacts, of power, of ancient lore. But the greatest power here, the one you truly sought to exploit, was Gladys's trusting nature. You preyed on her intellect, her curiosity, her desire for knowledge. You made her a sacrifice to your own insatiable greed."

The stranger shook his head, his breath coming in shallow gasps. "It wasn't greed," he insisted, though his voice lacked conviction. "It was... ambition. A desire to uncover the secrets that lie buried beneath the surface of our ordinary lives. Gladys shared that ambition. We were kindred spirits in that regard."

"Kindred spirits?" Finn's laughter was a harsh, broken sound. "She believed in your shared quest, your noble pursuit of knowledge. You believed in your ability to manipulate her, to use her as a conduit for your own selfish desires, and to discard her when the risks became too great. You saw her as a means to an end, a key to unlock treasures you could then claim for yourself."

The stranger's gaze fell to the polished sea glass O'Connell held. "That amulet... she gave it to me before the storm fully descended. She said it contained a fragment of the island's oldest song. She believed it would guide her, protect her. I... I took it. And I also took other items I had identified earlier, items that seemed to radiate a peculiar energy. Small, carved stones, fragments of pottery... things that she had been studying, but which I believed held the true significance."

He finally met O'Connell's steady gaze. "When the wave hit, and I saw her go under... I panicked. I stuffed everything into my satchel, the amulet included. I scrambled higher up the rocks, away from the relentless surge. I thought... I thought if I could just get away, I could then use the artifacts, the amulet, to understand what had truly happened. Perhaps even to... to prove I wasn't responsible."

"And instead, you've confessed to orchestrating her death," O'Connell stated, his voice a chillingly calm pronouncement. He gestured towards the open satchel lying by the stranger's feet. "Is that where you keep your treasures? The fruits of your deception?"

The stranger nodded, his shoulders slumping further. He made no move to defend himself, no attempt to flee. The fight had gone out of him, leaving only a hollow shell of a man.

As O'Connell moved to secure the satchel, the first rays of the rising sun broke through the clouds, bathing the cove in a golden light. The harsh edges of the rocks, the debris left by the storm, and the stark reality of the stranger's confession were laid bare. The storm that had raged throughout the night had been a tempest of nature, but the true storm, the one that had led to Gladys's demise, had been a storm of human ambition, deceit, and ultimately, a profound failure of empathy. The raw, exposed beauty of Cailleach's Embrace, usually a place of myth and mystery, now stood as a silent witness to a brutal betrayal. The evidence was undeniable, illuminated by the unforgiving light of dawn. The chase was over, but the true reckoning, for all involved, was only just beginning. The sea glass amulet, clutched in O'Connell's hand, felt heavy, a tangible symbol of Gladys's lost life and the dark secrets unearthed from the heart of the storm.

The Villages Reckoning

The first rays of dawn, weak and tentative, did little to dispel the heavy atmosphere clinging to Ballyknock. The storm had passed, leaving behind a bruised sky and an even more bruised community. O'Connell, his face etched with a weariness that went beyond physical exhaustion, watched as the villagers, drawn by the receding tide and the hushed urgency that had rippled through the night, began to emerge from their homes. Their eyes, accustomed to the solace of routine, now held a bewildered, fearful glint, as if the rising sun had revealed a truth they had long chosen to ignore.

The stranger, his confession echoing in the minds of those who had heard it whispered from the cove, was secured, a broken figure amidst the stark beauty of Cailleach's Embrace. But his capture was not an end; it was a catalyst. The true reckoning, O'Connell knew, would unfold not on the wind-swept shores, but within the very heart of the village, within the minds and hearts of its people.

He found Maeve by the old well, her face a roadmap of the generations that had drawn life from its depths. The news, carried on the dawn wind, had reached her with the swiftness of a struck bell. Her gaze met his, and in its depths, O'Connell saw not judgment, but a profound, sorrowful understanding.

"He spoke of Gladys," Maeve began, her voice low, resonant with the weight of unspoken history. It wasn't a question.

O'Connell nodded, the sea glass amulet still cool in his palm. "He confessed. The storm, her ambition... he used it all." The words felt inadequate, paltry against the enormity of what had happened.

Maeve sighed, a sound like the rustling of dry leaves. "We knew. Not the specifics, perhaps, not the chilling certainty of his intent. But we knew the island's allure. We knew the pull it exerted on those with a certain hunger for the unseen. And we knew the dangers of that hunger when left unchecked, unfettered by wisdom." She turned, her weathered hands gripping the rough stone of the well. "We chose silence. We chose to let the old stories hold sway, to allow fear to build higher walls than knowledge."

The elders, a council sworn to uphold the delicate balance of Ballyknock's isolation, gathered in the dim light of the village hall. The air was thick with unspoken recriminations, with the palpable weight of their collective failure. Liam, his usual jovial demeanor replaced by a grim solemnity, spoke first. "We've always been careful. Guarded. We never wanted outsiders to pry, to understand our ways, to... to exploit what we hold sacred."

"And in guarding, we became blind," Maeve countered, her voice carrying an authority that silenced Liam's protest. "We saw Gladys's fascination, her bright, inquisitive mind. We saw her delving into the old texts, the ones we keep locked away, the ones that speak of the island's pulse, its ancient power. We saw her seeking a deeper connection, a truth that resonated with something wild and untamed within her. And we said nothing."

Morrigan, her face usually serene, was troubled. "We feared the disruption. The questions. We feared that if we acknowledged the island's unique properties, its... vulnerabilities, then the outside world would descend. And that, we believed, would be the true destruction."

"But destruction found us anyway," Finn said, his voice raw with grief. "It came in the guise of one of our own, cloaked in the promise of shared knowledge. And our silence, our fear, it made Gladys a more tempting target. It made her an easier sacrifice." He looked at the elders, his gaze piercing. "You spoke of protecting sacred things. What is more sacred than a life? What is more sacred than the truth?"

The silence that followed was profound, broken only by the distant cry of a gull. It was the silence of a community confronting its own complicity, its own deeply ingrained habits of omission. They had built a fortress of secrecy, not to protect themselves, but to shield themselves from the uncomfortable responsibility of engaging with the world, of guiding those who, like Gladys, dared to look beyond the veil.

O'Connell felt the weight of their collective guilt settle upon him, a burden he hadn't anticipated. His task had been to apprehend a criminal, to uncover a truth. But now, he was a witness to the unraveling of a community, to the painful, necessary birth of a new understanding.

"The texts... they speak of more than just artifacts and power," O'Connell said, his voice steady, addressing the hushed assembly. "They speak of a responsibility. A covenant, perhaps, not just with the island, but with those who are drawn to its mystery." He held up the sea glass amulet. "Gladys believed this held a fragment of the island's oldest song. She sought harmony, understanding. She didn't seek to exploit; she sought to connect. And in her pursuit, she was betrayed."

Maeve stepped forward, her eyes meeting O'Connell's with a newfound resolve. "We have lived too long in the shadows of our own fears. We have allowed the whispers of the past to drown out the voices of the present. Gladys's life, though tragically cut short, has shown us the fallacy of our isolation. We cannot protect our secrets by burying our truths."

She turned to the villagers, her voice ringing with a clarity that resonated through the hall. "We have been custodians of a legacy, but we have failed to be guides. We have been guardians of silence, but we have neglected the power of understanding. From this day forward, we will learn. We will speak. We will honor Gladys not with hushed tones and averted gazes, but with an open heart and a willingness to share what we know, when it is sought with respect and sincerity."

Liam, his voice thick with emotion, added, "The world outside may not understand our connection to this island, our reverence for its wildness. But they will understand loss. They will understand truth. And perhaps, if we are honest, they will understand our desire to protect what is precious, even as we acknowledge our mistakes."

The path ahead was uncertain. The fragile understanding that had begun to dawn in Ballyknock was not a complete reconciliation, but a tentative step. O'Connell knew his report would have repercussions, that the outside world, once alerted to the island's unique nature, would inevitably seek to claim or control it. But for the first time, he felt a flicker of hope that Ballyknock, in its vulnerability, might find a way to navigate this new reality, not by retreating further into secrecy, but by embracing the messy, complicated process of engagement.

The reckoning within Ballyknock was far from over. It would be a slow, arduous process of dismantling generations of ingrained silence, of confronting the uncomfortable truths that lay buried beneath the surface of their placid existence. But as O'Connell looked out at the faces of the villagers, at the dawning of a new resolve in their eyes, he knew that the first, most crucial step had been taken. The echoes of the storm, and of Gladys's lost potential, would forever shape their future, but they would no longer be whispers of fear; they would be the resonating notes of a community finding its voice. The island's secrets, once guarded with a fierce, almost suffocating possessiveness, were beginning to breathe, to find their place not in the hidden corners of tradition, but in the broader, more complex tapestry of shared human experience. The sea glass amulet, now in O'Connell's keeping, was more than just evidence; it was a symbol of a life that had irrevocably changed the course of Ballyknock, a reminder that the greatest treasures often lay not in the artifacts themselves, but in the human connections that led to their discovery. The wind, which had carried whispers of suspicion and accusation, now seemed to carry a faint, nascent melody, a testament to the village's dawning courage, its hesitant embrace of a world it had so long sought to keep at bay.

O'Connell's Peace

The storm had passed, leaving behind the kind of profound stillness that often follows great upheaval. For Detective O'Connell, a quiet tide of resolution had begun to wash over him. The intricate puzzle of Gladys's demise, a tapestry woven from the wild threads of the Irish landscape, ancient lore, and the darker currents of human ambition, had finally yielded its secrets. It was a satisfaction that resonated deeper than mere case closure. It was the quiet hum of order restored, of truth, however painful, brought into the harsh light of day. He had come to Ballyknock seeking a perpetrator, a motive, a tangible answer to a chilling question. He found it, but he also found something far more elusive: a peace that settled not just upon the village, but within himself.

He found himself standing on the bluff overlooking Cailleach's Embrace, the same spot where the night had exploded in chaos and revelation. The sea, now a placid expanse of shifting blues and greys, lapped gently at the base of the cliffs. The jagged rocks, once stark silhouettes against a tempestuous sky, were now softened by the morning light, their ancient forms hinting at untold stories, at the enduring strength of the earth against the relentless erosion of time and tide. This rugged beauty, which had so recently been the stage for a tragedy, now felt different. It was still a place of sorrow, yes, but it was also a testament to resilience, to the enduring spirit that could emerge from the darkest of nights. The island's raw, untamed nature, which had both captivated Gladys and ultimately led to her undoing, now served as a poignant reminder of the delicate balance between allure and danger, between discovery and oblivion.

The intricate layers of the case had, in many ways, mirrored the complexities O'Connell had often wrestled with in his own life. The whispers of ancient magic, the subtle manipulations, the deep-seated traditions that both protected and imprisoned the community – it was a world apart from the sterile efficiency of the city precinct, yet the underlying human dramas were achingly familiar. Greed, obsession, the desperate yearning for something more, something transcendent, these were the forces that drove people, regardless of their setting. Gladys, with her bright, insatiable curiosity, had sought to understand the island's pulse, its hidden energies, and had been tragically misunderstood, her thirst for knowledge weaponized against her by a twisted ambition cloaked in feigned camaraderie.

He had witnessed the village's painful awakening, the slow, grudging dismantling of generations of protective secrecy. Maeve's words, echoing with the wisdom of the ages, had offered not a condemnation, but a path forward, a call to acknowledge the past, to learn from its failures, and to embrace a future where truth was not a threat, but a foundation. The elders, their faces etched with the weight of their collective responsibility, had begun the arduous process of bridging the chasm between their insular world and the wider one, a testament to the transformative power of confronting uncomfortable truths. Liam's grief had transformed into a quiet resolve, a promise to honor Gladys's memory not through silence, but through a nascent openness, a willingness to share the island's narrative with respect and sincerity.

O'Connell ran a thumb over the smooth, cool surface of the sea glass amulet he still carried. It was more than just a piece of evidence; it was a tangible link to Gladys, a reminder of her vibrant spirit and the profound impact she had, however inadvertently, on this remote corner of the world. She had sought connection, an understanding of the island's ancient song, and in her pursuit, she had inadvertently unearthed the darker melody of human betrayal. His role had been to uncover that betrayal, to bring the discordant notes into harmony with the truth, and in doing so, he had played his part in the village's own quiet resolution.

The allure of mystery, O'Connell mused, was a powerful force. It drew people in, beckoned them towards the unknown, promising revelation and wonder. But it also held a darker side, capable of ensnaring the unwary, of twisting genuine curiosity into dangerous obsession. Gladys had been drawn into that orbit, her passion for the island's secrets ultimately proving too potent, too seductive. He understood that pull, the relentless drive to peel back the layers, to find the hidden core of things. It was the same drive that had brought him to Ballyknock, the same drive that had defined his career.

The rugged coastline, with its dramatic cliffs and hidden coves, had always held a certain mystique. Now, having navigated its secrets, O'Connell saw it not just as a place of untamed beauty, but as a character in its own right, an ancient witness to the unfolding human drama. The wind, which had carried whispers of suspicion and accusation, now carried a faint, almost imperceptible melody, a testament to the village's dawning courage and its hesitant embrace of a world it had long sought to keep at bay. The resilience of the land, much like the resilience of the human spirit, was a profound and enduring thing.

He knew his report would ripple outwards, that the outside world, once alerted to the unique nature of this island, would inevitably seek to understand, perhaps even to control, what Ballyknock held so dear. It was a prospect that troubled him, the thought of the quiet sanctity of this place being disturbed by external forces. But he also knew that the village, having faced its own internal demons, had gained a newfound strength, a resilience that might just allow it to navigate these new currents with a measure of grace. They had learned to speak, to acknowledge their past, and in doing so, they had opened themselves to the possibility of a different future.

The peace O'Connell felt was not a triumphant, victorious peace, but a quiet, earned one. It was the peace of a completed task, of a storm weathered, of a difficult truth faced and acknowledged. He was a detective, a man whose life was dedicated to unearthing the concealed, to shining a light into the shadows. And in Ballyknock, he had found a place where those shadows had been particularly deep, particularly persistent. His role had been to pierce through them, not with brute force, but with a steady, persistent inquiry, guided by the echoes of a life lost and the quiet whispers of truth that always, eventually, found their way to the surface. The rugged beauty of the coast, once a stark backdrop to a grim investigation, now offered a sense of quiet contemplation, a reminder that even in the wake of profound loss, life, in its own persistent way, continued to find a way to bloom. The case of Gladys, and of Ballyknock, was closed, but its lessons, like the enduring rhythm of the sea, would continue to resonate within him.

The Legacy of Gladys Burton

The salty air, still carrying the tang of the recent tempest, now felt imbued with a new quality, a subtle shift in its resonance. It was the whisper of a story, a name that had once been a vibrant presence and was now becoming a legend. Gladys Burton. Her life, so abruptly extinguished on the storm-lashed shores of Ballyknock, had not simply ended; it had transformed, weaving itself into the fabric of the island's lore, becoming another chapter in the long, unfolding saga of Cailleach's Embrace. The raw, untamed beauty of this place, which had so profoundly drawn her in, now served as the eternal backdrop to her memory. The cliffs, the churning sea, the ancient stones – they had all witnessed her quest, her passion, and ultimately, her tragic end.

Detective O'Connell, as he stood on the bluff, felt the weight of this transformation. Gladys was no longer merely a victim, a case file to be closed. She was a spirit intertwined with the island's very essence. Her artistic soul, that insatiable hunger for beauty and meaning, had resonated deeply within this community, even if it had been tragically misunderstood by some. She had arrived with a sketchbook and an open heart, seeking not just inspiration, but a deeper connection to the ancient energies that pulsed beneath Ballyknock's surface. In her wake, she had left behind not just unanswered questions, but a quiet stirring within the hearts of those she had met, a subtle but undeniable challenge to the traditions that had long held the village in their gentle, yet firm, embrace.

The elders, those keepers of Ballyknock's soul, had spoken of Gladys with a newfound respect, their initial suspicion softened by the stark reality of her loss and the sincerity of her pursuit. They saw now that her fascination with the island's wild spirit was not a desecration, but a form of homage, a desperate attempt to bridge the gap between the modern world and the ancient mysteries they guarded. Maeve, in particular, had often found herself reflecting on Gladys's vibrant energy, the way she saw the world through an artist's eyes, finding art in the everyday, in the weathered faces of the fisherfolk, in the skeletal remains of boats pulled ashore, in the very patterns of the tide against the unforgiving rocks. Gladys's ability to capture the essence of Ballyknock, to translate its soul onto paper, had been a revelation, a mirror held up to the community, showing them a beauty they had perhaps taken for granted, or even begun to forget.

Liam, too, had spoken of Gladys with a quiet reverence. He remembered their conversations, often held under the vast, star-strewn sky, where she would talk of the island's 'song,' a mystical symphony she felt humming beneath the surface of everyday life. He had initially dismissed her theories as fanciful, the imaginings of an outsider captivated by local folklore. But now, with the clarity of hindsight, he understood. Gladys hadn't been chasing ghosts or fabricating legends. She had been listening, truly listening, to the island's ancient voice, a voice that had been present long before Ballyknock was even a name. Her journals, filled with vivid sketches and lyrical prose, were a testament to this profound connection. They were not just drawings; they were glimpses into her soul, reflections of the island's spirit as seen through her eyes.

These journals and sketches, O'Connell learned, had become more than mere mementos; they were being carefully preserved, treated with a reverence usually reserved for sacred texts. They were kept in a sturdy, sea-weathered chest, a gift from one of the older villagers, a tacit acknowledgement of Gladys's enduring presence. Within their pages lay the story of her journey, a narrative of discovery, of connection, and of a deep, abiding love for Ballyknock, a love that transcended even death. Her sketches captured the wild, untamed beauty of Cailleach's Embrace with an arresting intensity, imbuing each stroke with the very energy of the place. The wind-whipped heather, the stoic faces of the villagers, the swirling patterns of the sea – all were rendered with a life and vibrancy that spoke volumes of her empathy and her artistic prowess.

Her written words were equally evocative, filled with observations that went beyond the superficial. She wrote of the subtle shifts in the light, the moods of the sea, the ancient stories that seemed to cling to the very air. She described her attempts to understand the island's unique rhythm, its cyclical patterns of life and death, of creation and decay. There were passages that hinted at her growing unease, her sense of being watched, of a presence that was both alluring and subtly threatening. These entries, O'Connell felt, were crucial. They offered a glimpse into the psychological landscape of her final days, the growing intensity of her quest and the potential dangers it entailed. She had been seeking inspiration, a muse, but she had also, perhaps unknowingly, been stepping into a complex web of tradition and unspoken rules, a world where the boundaries between the physical and the spiritual, the real and the imagined, were profoundly blurred.

The community's decision to preserve her work was a significant step. It represented a conscious effort to integrate her narrative into their own, to acknowledge her contribution to the island's ongoing story. It was a testament to their evolving understanding, a willingness to embrace the outsider's perspective and to recognize the value of her artistic legacy. Gladys had, in her own way, forced them to look at their home with fresh eyes, to appreciate its enduring beauty and the deep history embedded within its very soil. Her art became a catalyst, a gentle nudge that encouraged them to re-evaluate their own relationship with their heritage, to find a balance between safeguarding their traditions and allowing them to evolve.

The journals served as a poignant reminder of the delicate tightrope Gladys had walked. She had been drawn to the mysteries of Ballyknock, to the whispers of the ancient past that permeated the island. She had sought to capture that essence, to translate it into a form that others could understand and appreciate. But in doing so, she had also brushed against something more powerful, something ancient and perhaps best left undisturbed. Her quest for inspiration had led her to the very edge of the island's secrets, to a place where the veil between worlds was thin, and where the consequences of intrusion could be profound. The sketches of the standing stones, the detailed renderings of the sea caves, the passionate descriptions of the island's folklore – all spoke of a woman deeply immersed in her subject, sometimes to her own peril.

O'Connell found himself contemplating the nature of inspiration itself. For Gladys, it was a consuming force, a driving passion that propelled her forward, even as it led her into increasingly perilous territory. She had sought to understand the 'song' of Ballyknock, to decipher its ancient melodies, and in her dedication, she had become part of that song herself. Her life and death were now interwoven with the island's narrative, a mournful yet beautiful harmony. The sea glass amulet, still cool and smooth in his pocket, was a tangible echo of her presence, a reminder of the vibrant spirit that had once inhabited this rugged landscape. It was a symbol of her quest, of her connection to the island, and of the ultimate price she had paid for her passion.

The preservation of her journals and sketches was more than just an act of remembrance; it was an act of reconciliation. It was the village's way of acknowledging that Gladys's journey, though tragically cut short, had not been in vain. She had brought a new perspective to Ballyknock, a way of seeing that had enriched their understanding of themselves and their home. Her art captured the wildness, the resilience, and the subtle, enduring magic of the island, qualities that were deeply ingrained in the lives of its inhabitants. She had seen the extraordinary in the ordinary, the mythical in the mundane, and in doing so, she had reminded them of the profound beauty that surrounded them daily.

The sketches of the local people, often depicted with a raw honesty that revealed their inner strength and their quiet dignity, were particularly moving. Gladys had not romanticized them; she had captured their essence, their resilience in the face of a harsh environment, their deep connection to the sea and the land. She had seen the stories etched into their faces, the wisdom in their eyes, the quiet determination that defined their existence. These portraits were not just likenesses; they were testaments to the human spirit, a celebration of the lives lived in this remote corner of the world.

Her exploration of the island's folklore, too, was evident in the pages of her journals. She had delved into the legends of the Cailleach, the ancient witch of winter, and the stories of the sea spirits, weaving them into her artistic vision. There were sketches of the standing stones, not just as geological formations, but as conduits of ancient power, imbued with a spiritual energy that Gladys clearly felt. Her interpretations, though filtered through her artistic sensibility, showed a deep respect for the oral traditions of Ballyknock, a desire to understand and to honor the beliefs that had shaped generations. She had sought to capture the intangible, the spiritual essence of the island, and in her art, she had come remarkably close.

The impact of Gladys Burton on Ballyknock was undeniable. She had arrived as an outsider, a fleeting visitor seeking inspiration, but she had left an indelible mark. Her quest for meaning had, in a profound and unexpected way, catalyzed a re-evaluation within the community. Her art and her journals served as a tangible legacy, a testament to her passionate spirit and her unique vision. They were a reminder that even in the quietest of places, the pursuit of beauty and understanding could spark profound change, forcing a community to confront its past, to acknowledge its traditions, and to embrace a future that was open to new interpretations, to new stories, to new whispers on the wind. The island, in its quiet way, had been touched by her presence, forever altered by the legacy of Gladys Burton. The delicate balance between seeking inspiration and respecting the profound mysteries that lay just beyond the horizon had been a journey Gladys had undertaken with all her heart, and one that had ultimately etched her into the very soul of the village.

The Enduring Mysteries of the Sea

The receding coastline of Ballyknock, a silhouette against the bruised dawn sky, held O'Connell captive for a long moment. The ferry's horn sounded, a mournful bellow that seemed to echo the very sentiments churning within him. He'd left a killer behind, a human hand responsible for Gladys's demise, and justice, in its most tangible form, had been served. Yet, as the emerald isle faded into the mists, O'Connell knew the true narrative of Cailleach's Embrace remained stubbornly, stubbornly unresolved. The island's spirit, the ancient force that had both drawn Gladys in and, perhaps, ultimately consumed her, was a far more complex adversary than any human. It was a mystery as vast and untamed as the Atlantic itself, a force that defied the neat conclusions of police reports and courtroom verdicts.

He clutched the sea glass amulet in his pocket, its familiar coolness a tangible link to the island and its ill-fated artist. Gladys had been captivated by this place, by its raw, untamed beauty and the undercurrent of ancient lore that pulsed beneath its surface. She had sought inspiration, a muse, and had found something far more profound, something that spoke to her soul in a language older than human words. Her journals, now carefully curated within the island's heart, were a testament to this journey. They were filled with sketches that weren't mere depictions of landscapes, but rather interpretations of the island's very essence, imbued with an almost visceral energy. The wind-battered cliffs, the tempestuous sea, the gnarled, resilient flora – she had seen them not just as elements of nature, but as living entities, participants in an age-old dialogue.

O'Connell recalled the villagers' initial apprehension towards Gladys, a skepticism born from centuries of tradition and a protective instinct towards their island's secrets. They had guarded their heritage fiercely, their lives intertwined with the rhythms of the sea and the whispers of the past. Gladys, with her outsider's curiosity and her artistic fervor, had represented a potential disruption to this delicate balance. Yet, her genuine passion, her evident respect for the island's spirit, had slowly chipped away at their defenses. They had seen in her sketches a reflection of their own home, seen through eyes that found beauty and significance in details they had perhaps long taken for granted. Her exploration of their folklore, her attempts to understand the Cailleach, the ancient winter deity, and the tales of sea spirits, had been met with a mixture of awe and trepidation. She had dared to peer behind the veil, to attempt to translate the intangible into something concrete, something that could be held and understood.

Maeve, the elder who had spoken with such quiet wisdom, had been particularly instrumental in bridging the gap between Gladys and the community. She had recognized in Gladys a kindred spirit, someone who felt the island's pulse, who heard its song. Maeve understood that Gladys wasn't seeking to exploit or sensationalize, but rather to connect, to understand the deep wellspring of spiritual energy that defined Ballyknock. Her own faith in the island's ancient ways, her knowledge of its hidden histories, had allowed her to offer

Gladys a guiding hand, a gentle illumination of paths that might otherwise have remained obscured. She saw Gladys's art not as a mere hobby, but as a sacred endeavor, a means of communicating the island's soul to a world that often seemed to have forgotten how to listen.

Liam, the young fisherman who had shared late-night conversations with Gladys, spoke of her as someone who had truly *listened* to the island. He described how Gladys had seen not just the danger in the sea, but its breathtaking beauty, its power, its constant state of flux. She had been fascinated by the way the waves sculpted the coastline, the way the tides ebbed and flowed with an almost conscious rhythm, the way the storms could transform the familiar landscape into something both terrifying and awe-inspiring. Her sketches of the churning sea, the crashing waves, the spray that kissed the very cliffs, were not just art; they were a testament to her profound respect for the ocean's raw, untamed power. She had understood that the sea was a force to be reckoned with, a primal energy that demanded both caution and reverence.

The preservation of Gladys's journals and sketches was a significant act for the villagers. It was an acknowledgement that her life, though tragically short, had not been without purpose. Her artistic legacy had become a part of Ballyknock's own unfolding narrative, a vibrant new thread woven into the ancient tapestry of the island. Her perspective, so unique and so deeply felt, had offered them a new way of seeing their home, a renewed appreciation for its enduring magic. They had seen themselves, their lives, their island, through her artistic lens, and in doing so, had been reminded of the profound beauty and resilience that characterized their existence. Her quest for inspiration had become, in a way, a quest for self-understanding for the entire community.

O'Connell knew that the human element of the crime had been resolved. The perpetrator, driven by greed and a misguided sense of entitlement, had been apprehended. But the deeper mystery, the enigma of Cailleach's Embrace, persisted. It was a mystery woven into the very fabric of the island, a story whispered by the wind and sung by the sea. Gladys had been drawn into this ancient narrative, captivated by its allure, and ultimately, she had become a part of it. Her quest had led her to the edge of something profound, something that existed beyond the realm of human comprehension, a place where the boundaries between the physical and the spiritual blurred into a magnificent, and sometimes dangerous, unknown.

The sea, O'Connell mused, was an eternal mystery. It held secrets as deep as its trenches, currents as powerful as its storms. It was a force of creation and destruction, a provider and a taker. Ballyknock, cradled by its embrace, was a microcosm of this duality. The island's spirit, the Cailleach's Embrace, was not a benevolent entity, nor a purely malevolent one. It was simply… potent. It was the raw, untamed essence of nature, a power that could inspire awe and wonder, but also demand a steep price from those who dared to pry too deeply. Gladys had been a seeker, an artist who yearned to understand the primal forces that shaped the world, and in her pursuit, she had touched upon something ancient and elemental.

As the ferry chugged further away, the island shrinking to a smudge on the horizon, O'Connell felt a profound sense of respect for the enduring power of the sea and the land. The case of Gladys Burton had been solved, but the larger mystery of Ballyknock, the captivating allure of its untamed spirit, remained. The sea would continue its ceaseless song, a haunting melody that would draw in other seekers, other artists, other souls yearning for connection with something primal and profound. And perhaps, in their own ways, they too would become echoes on the wind, forever intertwined with the island's ancient, enduring mystery. The knowledge that the human culprit had been brought to justice was a comfort, a necessary closure. But the enduring enigma of Cailleach's Embrace – its ancient spirit, its potent allure, its capacity for both breathtaking beauty and devastating destruction – that remained a profound and captivating mystery. The narrative concluded not with a neat resolution, but with the lingering, undeniable sense that the sea, and the secrets it so jealously guarded, would continue to capture and challenge those brave, or perhaps foolish enough, to listen to its ancient, haunting song. It was a timeless reminder of nature's awesome power, a power that transcended human understanding and ultimately, human comprehension. The waves crashed against the hull of the ferry, a percussive rhythm that seemed to carry the island's unspoken stories, stories that would continue to unfold long after O'Connell had returned to the bustling anonymity of the mainland. The spirit of Ballyknock, like the sea itself, was an entity that would forever remain at the heart of an enduring mystery.

AUTHOR'S NOTE

The realization of O'Connell's odyssey on Ballyknock is a testament to the contributions of numerous individuals. Leading the charge was the luminous essence of artist Gladys Burton; her fervent admiration for the island's untamed splendor and its ancestral narratives ignited this tale. My deepest appreciation extends to the invented inhabitants of Ballyknock, whose stoic fortitude and profound bond with their locale furnished the fertile ground for this cultural chronicle. Particular commendation is reserved for the conceived patriarchs and matriarchs, such as Maeve, the sixty-year-old custodian of local lore whose sagacity casts light upon the obscured, and the burgeoning spirits, like Liam, the forty-five-year-old publican whose gaze, reflecting the ocean's deep knowledge, discovers loveliness in the mundane. Lastly, profound gratitude is offered to my editor, whose discerning perception and astute recommendations refined the intricacies of this enigma, and to my kindred, for their steadfast encouragement and enduring understanding.

Ballyknock Folklore & Key Terms:

Cailleach's Embrace: Refers to the perceived spiritual essence or ancient power of Ballyknock island, often associated with the Cailleach, a winter deity in Celtic mythology. It embodies the island's wild, untamed nature and its profound, sometimes dangerous, allure.

Sea Glass Amulet: A personal talisman carried by Detective O'Connell, imbued with significance from his time on Ballyknock and his connection to Gladys Burton.

The Cailleach: An ancient Celtic figure, often depicted as a primordial goddess or hag associated with winter, storms, and the turning of the year. Her presence on Ballyknock is felt as a pervasive, elemental force.

Sea Spirits: Local beliefs in entities inhabiting the ocean around Ballyknock, influencing tides, weather, and the lives of the islanders.

Ferry Horn: A recurring auditory motif representing departure, transition, and the melancholic separation from Ballyknock.

Journals and Sketches: Gladys Burton's artistic record of her time on Ballyknock, offering a unique interpretation of the island's landscape, folklore, and spiritual undercurrents.

Ballyknock: The fictional island setting for the novel, characterized by its rugged coastline, ancient lore, and a potent, enigmatic spirit.

Cailleach: A mythical Celtic deity associated with winter, creation, and destruction, whose presence is felt as a powerful, elemental force on Ballyknock.

Ferry: A vessel used for transportation to and from Ballyknock, often symbolizing the boundary between the ordinary world and the island's mystique.

O'Connell: The protagonist, a detective tasked with investigating a crime on Ballyknock, who becomes increasingly drawn into the island's deeper mysteries.

Gladys Burton: A deceased artist whose fascination with Ballyknock and its ancient traditions forms a central element of the unsolved mystery.

Sea Glass: Small fragments of glass smoothed by the sea, often found on coastlines, sometimes used as talismans.

References:

Even though the tale of *Cailleach's Embrace* is a product of imagination, its deep resonance stems from the potent allure of Celtic lore and the raw, untamed might of the natural world. Imagine moonlight, a spectral veil, cast upon a secluded Irish cove where the relentless surge of the ocean pulverizes the ancient, unyielding rocks. This dramatic tableau, imbued with the very essence of elemental power, fuels the narrative's profound inspiration.

MacCulloch, John Arnott. The Religion of the Ancient Celts. Dover Publications, 2008. (Provides historical context for Celtic deities and beliefs.)

O'Curry, Eugene. Manners and Customs of the Ancient Irish. 1873. (Offers insights into Irish folklore and traditions.)

Monaghan, Patricia. The New Book of Goddesses and Heroines. Llewellyn Publications, 2014. (Explores archetypal figures in mythology, including winter deities.)

ABOUT THE AUTHOR

General observations on the Irish coastline and maritime folklore.

From his earliest days, Peter Hartwell has been drawn to the mysteries and the potent enchantment of the wild. His background, abundant with crafting intricate stories and exploring liminal spaces where the ordinary dissolves into the extraordinary, has honed his keen eye for detail and instilled a deep respect for atmospheric resonance. With the dramatic beauty of coastlines and the enduring echo of ancient lore fueling his creative engine, Peter strives to unveil the veiled histories embedded within our world. His newest creation, "Cailleach's Embrace," powerfully captures this burning passion, immersing readers in a captivating riddle where human grief and elemental forces intertwine. Peter makes his home in New York, near the tranquil expanse of Lake Erie.

Imagine "Cailleach's Embrace" unfolding beneath a celestial glow, where moonlight silvers a secluded Irish cove. The rhythmic roar of waves battering the ancient rocks forms a primal soundtrack to a narrative deeply concerned with the poignant intersection of profound human sadness and the raw, untamed energies that shape our existence. Hartwell, a resident of New York beside Lake Erie, has dedicated his life to excavating these hidden layers of reality, a pursuit evident in his lifelong fascination with enigmas and nature's wild heart. His previous endeavors, marked by the construction of complex narratives and explorations of the thresholds where the commonplace gives way to the miraculous, have gifted him with an incisive perception and a profound veneration for resonant atmospheres. Drawing sustenance from the raw grandeur of shorelines and the persistent hum of generational tales, Peter is driven to reveal the secret chronicles woven into the very tapestry of our shared existence.

Made in United States
North Haven, CT
19 October 2025

80985811R00113